The Ghost at Devils Tower

Carol Morosco
Philomine Lakota

Saguaro Books, LLC
SB
Arizona

Dedication

For the Lakota People
and in memory of Philomine Lakota

Years ago Native American children were banned from using their tribe's language in schools. They were expected to learn English. When this happened many Indian languages were forgotten and lost. Some of the children secretly spoke to each other using the native words learned from their parents and elders.

Philomine Lakota never forgot her tribe's language. She taught students at Red Cloud Indian School to speak in Lakota.

The Lakota words in this book were gifted to us by Philomine.

Chapter 1

Drum –*Čháŋčheǧa Kabúbu*

Ba-bum, bum. I can hear the sound of someone beating a native drum coming from the house as I walk along the sidewalk. Linda and Winnie must have gotten hold of Dad's drum. The windows are open, and I imagine arrows flying out of them, aimed at me. *Zip, zip, zip.* The arrows bring me to my knees. I drop my school backpack.

Mom opens the front door. "Anna, what are you doing out there?"

I don't tell her I had been imagining arrows knocking me down. She always says I let my imagination run away with me.

"Uh, nothing. Just dropped my backpack."

"Well, pick it up and come in. I need to run over to the nursery to check some orders. I've been waiting for you to come home to watch Linda and Winnie."

Oh, great, I wasn't planning on babysitting this afternoon.

Mom and Dad own Čhetáŋ's Nursery and Garden Center. Well, really Mom owns it and Dad does the ordering and works on the books. He also teaches a course called Native American Studies at the community college.

We are Native Americans. Lakota to be exact. We live in New Jersey, far from where our ancestors, who lived on the Great Plains. I am the oldest and my sister, Linda, is five. My mom and dad, Maisie and Oren, are proud Native Americans and they want Linda and me to feel the same way. Linda is clueless about most things. I guess that's because she's only five. And me, I'm OK about being Native. I just don't feel the need to tell everyone about it. I want to be a regular American kid with skinny jeans and my own phone.

I walk into the living room. Linda and Winnie are still banging on the drum.

"Come on, girls, tone it down," I say. Of course, they don't listen to me.

Linda giggles and plays louder. Winnie gives me her squinty glare, which is really something to see. She narrows her eyes to slits, pulls down her mouth, and stares at me. I call this her "snake-eye look". It's really scary, considering she's only eight and she can make herself look very mean.

8

Winnie Sandoz and her father, Vernon, are staying with us for a few days. Mr. Sandoz is meeting with my father. He wants my dad to go to South Dakota and teach a summer course at Oglala Lakota College. Winnie and her dad are Lakota natives, the same as us.

Dad says there are over 550 different Native American tribes living all over the country. Last summer, our whole family went out west on vacation. It was very cool. We saw clay houses where natives lived thousands of years ago and homes built into the sides of cliffs. I guess natives have lived here longer than anybody.

This summer we're staying at home and I have big plans with my best friend, Liz.

"Anna, I'll be back in about an hour," explains Mom. "Give the girls some fruit if they ask for a snack." She grabs her purse and heads for the door.

"OK," I say.

Linda and Winnie huddle together on the sofa. They are not drumming now. They are whispering to each other. Not a good sign.

"You heard what Mom said," I remind them. "Fruit for a snack."

Linda smiles. Winnie shoots me her snake-eye look. I can't wait for her to go home. *It won't be long now*, I think.

I go to my room, drop my backpack and flop on my bed. Tomorrow is the last day of school and I can't wait. Liz and I have planned out our whole summer. I'm finally going to get a phone of my own.

Last year, I was hoping to get a phone for my birthday. I certainly dropped enough hints about wanting one. Did I get one? Nope. Instead, my mom gave me an antique stone bracelet that had been handed down from mother to daughter for centuries. It has a chipped stone on it and looks ancient. Not shiny and modern, like a new phone.

On my birthday, Mom, Dad, and Linda came into my room, sang to me, and handed me the wrapped present with big smiles on their faces. I was still hoping the box contained a phone. After I opened it, I forced myself to give a big smile.

I said, "Wow. This is great."

I thought, *where is my phone?*

Now, though, I have a great plan. I'll have a phone by the end of the summer. Liz's mom owns a dog walking business. She said she would pay Liz and me to walk the dogs in the morning. She would do the afternoon and evening. I told my dad about the job. I mentioned I would have enough money to buy a phone.

He smiled. "You do realize, Anna, that it's not just the phone you have to pay for. There will be monthly charges too."

Talk about a kick in the stomach. "I do. And I've planned to pay for those."

I didn't have a plan, but I'd worry about that later. I did have one concern. It was about Liz.

"Anna, let's walk the dogs past Jason's house," said Liz.

"Why? That's four blocks extra."

"I think he's cute," answered Liz.

10

Now, anyone who met Jason would wonder about Liz. Jason is in my history class. He slouches in his seat and puts his feet in the aisle so no one can get past. You have to walk down another aisle and approach your desk from the back of the room. His hair covers his face. I wonder what's under there. He coughs loudly whenever anyone answers a question. He says he has allergies when the teachers tell him to stop.

Liz is my best friend, though and she helped me get this job. If she wants to walk past his house every day, we'll walk past his house every day. Maybe he'll cough out the window at us. I don't care. I'm getting my own phone. Liz and I also plan on going to the community pool every day after walking the dogs. It's going to be the best summer ever,

Bang, Bang, Earth to Anna. Something is happening downstairs. I jump off the bed and run down. No one is in the living room. Another "bang" in the kitchen. I walk in to see an overturned chair on the floor. Winnie is helping Linda up.

"What's going on here?" I ask. As if I didn't know they were doing something not permitted by Mom.

"We were trying to get the chips down from the cupboard," says honest Linda.

"I think we were looking for fruit," chimes in Winnie. She elbows Linda.

"Yeah, right," I answer. "That's where everyone keeps the fruit. Try the refrigerator."

Winnie gives me her snake eyes. Just then, the front door bangs open. Mom's back but not the happy, relaxed Mom who left the house. I can tell something is wrong.

Mom sits down at the kitchen table. "Winnie, girls come sit."

Uh-oh, I think. *Here comes some bad news.* We sit down, and Mom reaches for Winnie's hands.

"Winnie, I just got a call about your grandma," says Mom.

Winnie starts to breathe hard. Her hands are shaking.

"She's had a fall and is in the hospital," explains Mom. "She's going to be OK but she will have to stay in the hospital for a few days. Your dad's making plans right now to return home."

"Is it my grandma's bad leg? She broke it once before. It's very weak. She has trouble walking on it and needs a cane."

"I'm not sure, honey," replies Mom. "Your dad will be here soon and will explain everything to you."

I ask, "Should we help Winnie pack up?"

Mom answers, "Winnie will be staying with us while her dad gets everything settled back home. He's flying out tonight.

"Girls, we'll be taking Winnie back home in that your Dad will be going out there anyway to teach at the Lakota College."

Mom reaches over and gives Winnie a hug.

Then, my summer plans go up in native smoke. I want to scream.

I slouch in my chair and start to cough.

Chapter 2

Grandma – *Uŋčí*

I can't believe my luck. Here it is the last day of school and I should be celebrating with Liz and my friends. Instead, I had to tell Liz all our plans are off. I can't walk the dogs with her. I won't earn any money. I still won't have a phone. She'll ask another girl to dog walk with her. I'll probably lose a best friend too. Can life get any worse?

At home, Linda's hopping around doing a native dance. She's so happy Winnie is staying with us. She can't wait to go out west to see Winnie's home. All I've heard since Winnie came to visit is how beautiful her home is, how wonderful her pool is, how many toys and electronics fill her bedroom and how she has everything we don't have. She tells us every day.

Linda says, "Winnie lives in a mansion. Winnie is rich."

I'm sick of hearing about Winnie. She isn't nice to me.

One time, I caught her looking through my dresser drawers. I opened the door to my room and saw her with my stone bracelet in her hand. I asked her, "What are you doing?"

She said, "I'm looking for some paper and a pen."

"In my dresser? In my private room?"

She dropped the bracelet, ran to the bathroom and locked the door. I could hear her crying in there.

I went to get Mom. I told her what happened. Mom immediately went to the bathroom and called to Winnie. "Winnie, honey, it's OK. Open the door, and we'll talk about it. Anna's out here and she wants to apologize for yelling at you."

What? I have to apologize to Winnie for sneaking into my room and going through my things?

"Tell Anna, to go away. Then I'll come out," said Winnie.

"Fine. I'm going." I couldn't believe what I was hearing. Mom was on her side.

I waited in the kitchen to see what would happen. Mom finally came down and said she wanted to talk to me.

"OK but I hope I'm not in trouble because I didn't do anything wrong."

"Anna, Winnie is having a hard time. She worries about her grandma. Life isn't easy for her," began Mom.

"It isn't easy for me either," I exclaimed.

"Anna, you have a mother, father and sister. Your family is complete. Don't you think Winnie would like that too?"

"She has her grandma and her dad. Where's her mother?" I asked.

"Winnie's mother died when she was a baby. Her grandmother has been taking care of her; however, her grandma is old and not well. I think Winnie helps to take care of her grandma. She told me she does some of the cooking and cleaning. That's a lot of responsibility for an eight-year-old. She's not much older than Linda."

"Well, I can't imagine Linda taking care of us. We would have cookies for every meal."

"Anna, try to understand Winnie a little better. I see how she acts around you. I think she admires you and wishes you were her big sister," concluded Mom.

"I don't know about that, Mom." I thought about Winnie's squinty eyes and mean face. *I'm not convinced Winnie likes me.*

"OK Mom. I'll try to see things from her point of view."

"Thanks Anna. That's all I can ask," sighed Mom.

Here I am sitting in class. Everyone is signing each other's yearbook. Everyone is talking about their summer plans, except for me. I glance up and see Liz laughing and talking with Stacy. She doesn't even like Stacy. She said she was too bossy. They're probably making plans for walking the dogs.

We're all just waiting for the dismissal bell. I glance at the clock. We still have thirty minutes to go. I can picture Linda and Winnie at home, maybe, beating on the drums again. Then I remember how Winnie likes to go through my things. I sit straight up. I feel a panicky feeling spread across my chest. Winnie might be tempted to explore my room again. Oh, no, She might find my most precious and scary treasure of all the twig horse. I look at the clock again. The hands are moving so slowly. I have to get home at once. If she finds that horse, it could be a disaster. I watch the clock again. Why does it move so slowly? I really need to get home now.

I raise my hand. "Miss Henry, can I talk to you?"

"Yes, what is it, Anna?"

I walk up to the teacher's desk with my arms folded over my stomach. I put my head down, trying to look sick.

"I'm not feeling well. I wonder if I can leave now?"

"Anna, the bell rings in ten minutes. I'm sure you can wait for that."

No, I can't, I think. "OK," I say.

Finally, the bell rings. Everyone jumps up and heads to the door.

I try to push my way to the front. It doesn't work. I tell myself to relax and to breathe slowly. It will be OK. I head toward the hallway.

"Anna, wait for me," calls Liz.

I turn and see her waving for me to stop. *I have to stop. She'll be mad if I don't.* She catches up to me. We must look funny, walking side by side. Liz is the opposite of me. She is tall and thin with long blond hair and blue eyes. I, on the other hand, am short and have black hair and eyes. My Dad says we are built like natives with sturdy bodies. I'm still hoping I'll outgrow "sturdy".

"Anna, why are you running so fast?"

"I have to get home to help my mom with the girls. She has to go to work," I say. That's another problem of mine. Lies just slide off my tongue. I don't want to lie but how would I ever explain the twig horse? No one would ever believe me.

"Anna, I was hoping you could come to my house for lunch then we could go to the pool." Liz pouts a little.

I'm happy she wants to invite me over even though I can't do dog walking with her. She's not mad at me. That's super good but I must get home right now.

"Liz, I wish I could go to your house, too, but my mom will be mad if I'm not home to help her. I'll call you later," I promise.

"All right. Remember to call. I want to tell you what Jason wrote in my yearbook. You're going to freak out. It's so great," says Liz.

Blah, blah, blah. Old Jason. I can hardly wait. Maybe he wrote, "Cough, cough, cough" in her book. Liz is so smart. What does she like about him?

I run all the rest of the way home. My heart is beating so hard. I slam the front door behind me. I run upstairs to my room. All of my drawers have been opened and some have been emptied.

"What's been going on?" I scream.

"Anna, lower your voice," demands Mom. She is carrying a suitcase into her bedroom.

"Mom, where are my clothes and my things from my drawers?"

"Oh, Anna, Linda, and Winnie wanted to surprise you. They packed your clothes for our trip out west. Please remember to thank them."

"Where are the girls?"

"I think they're in the garage helping Dad."

My heart is in my mouth. I run downstairs and out the door.

Linda is putting her pool stuff in the open trunk of the car.

"Hi, Anna. We packed for you," Linda says.

I look at Winnie. She just smiles and says, "We sure did."

Now what?

Chapter 3

Buffalo – *Tȟatȟáŋka*

I walk over to the car. The trunk is filled with suitcases and bags of extra stuff. One bag has all Linda's favorite stuffed animals, the ones she can't sleep without.

"Hi, girls. Mom said you packed everything for me," I say.

"Yes, Anna, we put in your shorts, tops and a bathing suit for Winnie's pool," says Linda.

I look over at Winnie. She is nervously biting her nail and jiggling her leg. *Now, why is she nervous?* I wonder. Did she find the twig horse in my room? If she did, she would put it in her suitcase. I'm sure about that. I can't just ask her because what if she didn't find it? If I bring it up, she'll want to know all about it.

"Thanks," I reply. "I'm going back inside to make sure I have everything I need."

Dad calls out, "Anna, look at the trunk. I don't think we can fit one more thing in there."

He's right. I think the whole back of the car looks like it will drag on the road.

"I'm just going to see about my toothbrush and some little things like that," I promise.

"Make sure of it," says Dad.

I go back inside and head straight to my room. The twig horse should be in the dresser's second drawer. After I found it in the attic I carefully wrapped it in tissue paper using one hand and I taped it to the back of the drawer. I haven't touched it since.

I immediately see the girls had emptied some clothes from the second drawer. I reach into the back of the drawer. Whew. It's still there taped to the wood. They didn't find it. I gently pull at it. The wrapped-up twig horse is in my hand again. Now, what to do?

"Anna, are you upstairs?" calls Mom. "Dad's waiting. He wants to get on the road. We have an awfully long drive. The sooner we get started, the better."

"Just a minute," I yell so she can hear. "I'm packing my toothbrush and some other stuff. I'll be right down."

I make a quick decision. I'll take the twig horse with me. That way, I'll always know where it is. I go to the bathroom to get a red travel bag I keep under the sink. In goes the horse, my toothbrush, and toothpaste. I decide to throw in my stone bracelet. I head downstairs.

Oh, drat it. I remember I promised to call Liz. This is ridiculous. That's why I want my own phone. I could call her from the car while we are driving.

"Let's hurry, Anna," says Mom.

"Mom, I have to make a quick call to Liz. I promised her."

"Well, don't talk too long. The girls are getting restless."

I call Liz from the kitchen. I tell her we're leaving for South Dakota. She fills me in on what Jason wrote in her yearbook. He wrote, "Liz, you're cool. Jason." She's so excited.

She's sure it means something important. I'm glad this makes her happy. Part of me is glad I'm not dog walking past his house every morning. I don't think he's cool.

Mom is still in the kitchen making sandwiches to take for lunch when I go outside to join the others. Linda and Winnie are rolling a ball back and forth under the car. Dad keeps telling them to stop but the game goes on.

"What do you think of that, Anna?" asks Dad. He points to the bumper of the car. I can see he has put a sticker on it. It says, **Bridge the Divide**. He steps back and admires his work.

"What does "Bridge the Divide" mean?" I ask.

"It means come together."

"Who's coming together?"

"Well, the past and the present. Old cultures and new cultures. Your tribe and my tribe. We bridge the divide and move forward together. That's what it means," explains Dad.

I still don't get it. How do we do it? "Sounds good," I say.

"It's better than good. It's the way we should live," declares Dad.

I think it's time for me to let it go. "OK. When are we leaving?" I ask and with that, Mom comes out, holding the lunch bag. She locks the front door. We get in the car and South Dakota here we come..

It's not easy being in the back seat with a five and an eight-year-old. Mom makes me sit in the middle for the first part of the drive so they can play their "truck game". Winnie and Linda look out their windows and try to be the first to spot a truck. Whoever sees a truck and yells, "Truck," first gets to add a point to their score. Do you know how many trucks are on the road? Doesn't anyone buy cars these days? My head is throbbing by the time we stop for gas. Even dad is shaking his head. He doesn't want to say anything because Winnie is a guest.

I don't feel that way. "Girls, play another game. I have a headache."

Winnie rolls her eyes at a giggling Linda. I sigh. *This is going to be an awfully long trip.*

We have to stop at motels along the way. It will take several days to reach South Dakota. The scenery changes along the way. We leave crowded roads and land dotted with houses and little towns.

Soon, open space and flat prairie lands are all we see. The ground is covered with different grasses.

Mom points out, "Look there, girls. That's sweet grass. There's sagebrush and notice how the grasses are different heights. The prairie might look empty but there are thousands of animals in there living off the grasses and bushes."

The flat land rolls on and on. When we stop to fill the gas tank, Linda notices little holes in the yard next to the station. Just then, a tan head pops out of the hole.

Linda screams," Look, look at that. Oh, it's so cute. It's like a big hamster. Can I pet it?"

"I wouldn't get too close," warns Dad. "Those are wild animals called prairie dogs. They dig out those holes then live in them."

"I'm not afraid of them. They're little," replies Linda.

"Listen to your Dad. There are lots of wild animals out here. They would attack you because they are frightened of you," says Winnie.

"All right but they are cute," says Linda.

We settle back in the car. I have the window side at last.

Mom asks, "Who wants some lemonade?"

Pass me some coffee, please, extra strong. I know I won't get that but I can dream. "I'll have some lemonade," I say.

The girls nod off, and finally it's quiet in the car. I watch out my window and notice the land is changing again. It is drier and sandier with just patches of grass then I see them. Brown and large with giant heads, all grazing together, buffalo. I jump up in my seat.

"Look, look over there." I point to the herd.

My father pulls the car to a stop. The girls wake up. All heads are turned toward the buffalo.

"The buffalo has always been a sacred animal to the Lakota tribe," begins Dad. "Years and years ago, the tribe depended on the buffalo, they called *thatȟáŋka*, for almost everything needed in life. The buffalo provided hide for the *thípi*, clothing and blankets. Its bones made knives, shovels, arrowheads, and more. Its horns made cups, spoons and toys. Even the tail was made into a whip. They didn't waste one part of the buffalo after it was killed and they never killed more than they needed for the tribe.

"The Lakota lived in houses called *thípi*, tent-like houses that could be moved from place to place as they followed the buffalo herds. They would work together as a group to track and kill the animal. Before they started out, they would offer a prayer to the Great Spirit called *Wakȟáŋ Tȟáŋka*. They would thank him for the buffalo he would provide for their people."

Linda interrupts. "Do the Lakota still hunt the buffalo and live in a *thípi*?"

Winnie answers, "No. We live in houses and have jobs just as you do."

"Oh, that's too bad." Linda sighs. "I would like to live in a thípi but I wouldn't hunt the buffalo. I would have one for a pet."

We all laugh, even Winnie. Suddenly, Winnie looks out the window and sits up straight. She starts biting her nail again. We pass a sign that reads **Pine Ridge**.

Dad says, "Winnie, you're home now." Winnie starts breathing fast. She jiggles her leg. She looks as if she is going to be sick. What is so wrong about coming home?

Chapter 4

Horse – *Šúŋkawakȟaŋ*

Pine Ridge Reservation is located south of the Black Hills and the Badlands. On the north side, the Black Hills are all dark with trees. In between the Badlands are canyon-like cliffs with red stripes running through them.

"This is beautiful," murmurs Mom, as she twists her head from side to side.

We drive down a dusty road toward Pine Ridge. We see small ranch houses on large areas of land.

"Look at all the horses and cows," points out Linda.

"Those are cattle," says Winnie. "They graze on the open fields."

I look over at Winnie to see if she is still biting her nails. No, she's stopped being nervous. Still, she doesn't look happy to be home. She looks sad and resigned.

"I know why the hills are called black," announces Linda.

"The trees look black from here."

I sigh. She's only five and she's already "Queen of the Obvious."

"Yes," replies Dad. "Not only that but the Black Hills, called *Páha Sápa*, are very sacred and important to the Lakota Tribe. Years ago, the government seized the hills for the new settlers coming to live out west. The Lakota and other Sioux tribes are trying to get the land back. They've even been offered one billion dollars from the government for the hills but they refuse to take the money. They simply want their own land given back to them."

"Why? That's a lot of money," I say.

"The Black Hills are the sacred center of the world for the Lakota. We believe the first Lakota came up from the ground through the wind cave. We don't want to sell the land of our ancestors," explains Dad.

"Winnie, are we getting closer to your house?" asks Mom.

"Yeah, we're almost there," says Winnie. She drops her head and folds her arms over her chest.

"Winnie, tell me when you see your house," says Dad.

We travel a little farther down the road when Winnie points her finger to the left. "That's it," she says.

A small tan house sits in a dusty yard. There's one tree to the side of it and a view of a fenced-in area in the back. A line of drying clothes is on the other side. Some tires are piled up by the entrance to the dirt driveway. I think, *This is not a mansion.*

Linda bursts out, "This can't be your house, Winnie. It's too small."

"Hush, Linda," warns Mom. "It's just the right size for a home."

We park in the driveway and get out of the car. Dad starts to unload the trunk. Winnie's dad, Vernon, comes out the front door. He extends his arms and says with a big smile, "Welcome, Chetáŋ family."

Dad shakes his hand and says, "It was a long trip but we traveled through some beautiful country."

Linda breaks away from the group and heads toward the open front door. "I want to see the pool," she announces. Linda runs into the house.

She doesn't hear Winnie's soft voice say, "Wait, Linda, please."

The adults stand talking about the trip. Winnie and I are frozen in the yard. We're waiting for Linda and what I suspect is going to be more disappointment. There won't be a pool.

Suddenly, we hear a happy scream of surprise, "Yeah, wahoo," Linda barrels out the front door. She runs to hug Winnie. "This is the best ever, why didn't you tell me, Winnie?"

I can't wait for Winnie to speak. "Tell you what, Linda? What?"

"Winnie has her own horse; it's in the back yard. What's his name, Winnie? Is he tame? Can I ride him? Can you teach me how to ride a horse? Can I help you…?"

"Slow down, Linda. Take a breath," says Mom.

Linda is so excited about the horse she has completely forgotten about the pool. I look over at Winnie. She seems relieved.

Vernon grabs a suitcase and says, "Let's not stand out here in this hot sun. Come into the house. I want to introduce you to my mother."

Dad, Mom and I pick up the rest of the suitcases and follow Vernon into the house. It's dark inside. The curtains are pulled tight against the sun's rays. There's one sofa covered with a native patterned blanket and two bent twig rocking chairs that remind me of my little twig horse. There aren't many pictures on the walls. There are a map and some old school pictures of a younger Winnie.

"I'm going to sleep on the sofa," says Vernon. "You folks follow me to the bedrooms."

We move down a dark hallway. My parents turn right into Vernon's room and drop the suitcases. I follow him to the left. We arrive at the second bedroom. There are bunk beds and one single bed.

"Here we are," sings out Vernon. "You girls will all be nice and cozy here." He drops the bags on the floor and leaves.

I stand in the middle of the room. It's small. We'll be tripping over each other. I'm not taking one of the bunk beds. I dump my bag on the single bed. I think we'll be cozy all right.

"Hello, hello," a voice calls out.

I follow the sound of it down the rest of the tiny hall into the third and final bedroom. I stick my head through the doorway.

"Hello. Who are you?" asks a little old lady wrapped in a red, yellow, and black striped blanket.

I think she must be sweating under that blanket. "Hi, I'm Anna Čhetáŋ. We brought Winnie back home from New Jersey."

"Oh, my, such a long trip for you to make. Such a kind thing to do," she says. She reaches out her hand to touch me.

"I'm Winnie's grandma. My Lakota name is Red Moon, but I am called Ruby. I'm sorry I can't get up to welcome all of you. My leg is not doing so well."

"No, no, no. Please stay in bed. I'll go and get my family to come to see you."

"Thank you, Anna."

I retrace my steps down the hall and turn right into the kitchen. I look around. There's a small wooden table with four chairs. I don't think we'll all be able to sit down there for meals. The rest of the kitchen looks like every other kitchen except there's no dishwasher. It has an old stove and refrigerator. There are no cupboards. Instead, there are shelves that hold dishes, pots, and pans and food things, such as cans and cereal boxes.

On the counter is a statue of a brown horse. It looks hand carved. It's small, the size of an apple. It reminds me of my twig horse, even though it's not made the same way. I think of my horse, safe in my red bag.

I look out the small window over the sink. It faces the back and the fenced-in yard. There's Linda already up on the horse. Winnie is holding the bridle strap and leading the horse and Linda around the yard. Linda is smiling from ear to ear. Her dream has come true, an animal, a pet, she can love.

My sister loves animals. My dream is a cell phone. Her dream is a pet of her own. Linda sees every animal as a potential pet. She doesn't care what kind of animal it is. She wants to bring it home and take care of it. A kitten, a puppy, a bird, a hamster, a grasshopper, an ant; it doesn't matter, Linda Čhetáŋ loves it. She begs Mom and Dad for a pet.

Their answer is always the same: "Linda, when you are older and can take care of one then, you'll have one."

I am sure Linda thinks she'll have one by the time she's six. I'm sure my parents have a later date in mind, such as when she's thirty and out of the house. This doesn't stop Linda from adopting all kinds of inappropriate pets.

I remember the time we stayed at the lake for two weeks. We had our own dock and a small boat. Dad brought fishing poles and gear with him. He was going to teach us to fish. A grand Lakota tradition, he kept saying.

Standing on the dock with our poles and hooks ready, Dad showed us how to thread a worm on the hook. The first scream brought Mom running from the cabin. She thought Linda had punctured herself on the hook. Linda was jumping up and down, yelling, "Stop. Stop. Stop."

"Oren, what are you doing? Is she hurt?" Mom was confused because Dad wasn't standing next to Linda.

"No, Maisie, she doesn't want me to put the worm on the hook," said a frustrated Dad.

"He's hurting it." Linda sobbed as if she were on the hook.

"Oh, Linda, I don't think fishing is for you." Mom put her arm around Linda and led her back to the cabin. Linda cried all the way.

Mom called over her shoulder, "Anna, you can learn how to fish from your Dad. Linda's done."

Great, I thought. *Be a native and weave worms.*

A couple days later, we all noticed an awful stench coming from the porch. We all stood out there, trying to figure out what it was.

"Oren, you took out the garbage, didn't you?" asked Mom, wrinkling her nose.

"Yes, of course I did," answered Dad.

We walked in circles around the porch. At last, I noticed a covered can in the corner. "It's coming from there," I said, holding my nose.

"No, no, those are my pets," said Linda, running to the can.

"Honey, let me see," said Mom gently prying the can from her hands.

It was disgusting. A can of worms, most of them dead.

"I just wanted some pets and Daddy was going to let the fish eat them," Linda cried.

"It's all right, honey. One day we'll get you a bigger pet," said Mom.

Here we are; Linda loves Winnie's horse. Who wants to bet that's the pet she'll want? Again, I think about my twig horse. *I'm sure I won't use it out here. Well, I'm fairly sure.*

Chapter 5

Stars – *Wičháȟpi*

Everyone comes in to say hello to Winnie's grandma. We all squeeze into the tiny bedroom.

"I'm so happy to see all of you," says Ruby. "Thank you so much for taking such good care of our Winnie. I don't know what I'd do without this girl." She gives Winnie a smile and moves to hold her hand.

"She was no problem at all," says Mom. "We're glad we could help you and Vernon out."

I look from Mom to Winnie. I think *Mom doesn't really know Winnie as I do. Maybe she'll find out by the end of this visit.*

The dinner seating arrangement works out OK. Winnie sits in Ruby's room and eats with her grandma. Vernon pulls up a stool to the kitchen table and eats dinner with us.

We have something incredibly good for dinner. Vernon makes native fried bread and puts cooked meat, onions, peppers, and corn on top of it. He calls it a "native taco." I won't mind having more of them. After dinner, we clear the table and wash the dishes. I already miss the dishwasher back home.

"It's been a long day," says Dad, stretching his arms while yawning. "I need to get some sleep. Tomorrow I'll check in with the college. I have paperwork to fill out and I'm anxious to meet the summer staff."

"Mom, can I sit outside with Winnie for a little while? I want to watch Winnie brush Red Paint," says Linda.

I must be tired too. As I ask the question, I already know the answer; "Who's Red Paint?"

"Winnie's horse," answers Linda, while shaking her head at my ignorance.

"Oh, yeah, of course," I say.

I go to my shared room and try to organize my things into the one drawer I've been given in the three-drawer dresser.

It's tight. Now, where do I hide the red bag with the twig horse? I look around the room. Not in the drawer. Not under my pillow and there's no closet. Where, where, where? I look up, down, left, right, trying to find a spot. Then I see it. Up at the roofline, there's a wide beam stretching across the width of the room. If I can reach it, I can slide the bag on it and it won't be seen from down below.

I tiptoe to the door and listen. No one is in the hallway. I drag the dresser to the middle of the room. I stand on my bed and step up on the dresser. The red bag is in my hand. I slide it on top of the beam and jump down.

"There," I say, as I rub my hands together to get the dust off.

"There, what?" asks Winnie appearing out of nowhere. "Why is the dresser in the middle of the room?" She stares at me.

She has her snake eyes again. Wow, it's her mean look and her "what are you doing?" look. One scary look for many things. I'm impressed.

"Oh, yeah, um, I was just seeing if I moved the dresser would it give us more space in here." I know it's a lame answer but that's all I could think of on short notice.

Winnie looks at me as if I'm two years old. "This isn't going to work. Linda and I have no room to get into our beds."

She looks as if she's going to say, "Duh," but doesn't. She should. I deserve it.

Winnie glances up at the beam and down at me. I know what she's thinking. I have to get the bag down. Winnie helps me push the dresser back to the wall.

I ask, "Winnie, do you mind leaving the room? I want to change my clothes."

She hesitates a moment. "Sure."

When the door is closed, I move the dresser back under the beam and pull down the red bag. I blow the dust off it and put it under my mattress. I can't keep it there for long. I've seen enough TV to know everyone searches under mattresses first to find valuables. I'll have to find a better hiding place later. I change my shorts and wander out to see what everyone is doing.

Mom, Vernon, Linda and Winnie are sitting out back on wooden benches. They're all looking up.

I wonder what they are looking at.

I sit down next to Mom and look up too. What greets my eyes is unbelievable, Millions, no billions, no, maybe trillions of stars cover the night sky. They look to be art store glitter dumped over the darkness.

"This is great, is it always this way?" I ask.

"Pretty much, except when it's cloudy or rainy," answers Vernon.

"Wow. Mom, how come we can't see stars this way at home?" I ask.

"We have light pollution, Anna," says Mom.

"What's light pilubtion?" asks Linda.

"Light pollution," corrects Mom, "is all the light from towns, cars, stores, lamp posts and even houses, which lights up the sky and stops the light of the stars from reaching us. Out here on the plains, we can see the stars clearly because there are fewer people here lighting up the streets and countryside."

"Lakota believe when you die your spirit leaves your body and becomes a star in the heavens. We believe our relatives, our uncles, our aunts, our parents and all our family who have died are up in the sky looking down on us. We believe we can call on them to watch over us and to help us when we need them to," says Vernon.

"Dad," says Winnie, "Mom is a star in the sky. Right, Dad?"

"Yes, Winnie, her spirit has never left us. I feel her love for us every day and when I look up at the stars, I see one that seems to twinkle and shine brighter than all the others. I'm sure that star is your mom."

I look over at Winnie. Her eyes are searching the night sky for that one special star.

"Which one is it, Dad?" she asks.

Vernon points up over the roof. "It's the one over our house. She never goes far away."

We all look straight up. I think I can see it. Winnie stares at it holding her hands over her heart. I hope Winnie's star mother sends a ray of light right to Winnie. We sit for a while longer in quiet. Then, thud, Linda falls off the bench.

Mom picks up Linda. "She's sound asleep. I'll take her in to bed."

Soon, everyone yawns and decides bed sounds to be a good idea, too. I hurry to the room while Winnie is in the bathroom. I slide my hand under the mattress to check on the twig horse. It is where it should be.

Soon the house is dark and all is quiet. I toss and turn in my bed. I just can't get comfortable. I reach under the mattress and feel for the red bag. I pull it out.

What am I doing? Don't do it. It's too dangerous out here. Something terrible will happen.

Chapter 6

House – *Thípi*

I can feel the outline of the twig horse through the cloth bag. It's so small and yet so powerful. I found it in the attic right before Winnie and her dad came to stay with us. Dad had asked me to go up to the attic to bring down his drum. He keeps very old native things, such as arrowheads, clothes and painted bowls in a trunk. He uses these things when he teaches at the college. When I opened the trunk I saw a cardboard box tied with dirty yellow string at the bottom peeking out from under a faded rug. I slid the string off and opened the box. Inside was a stick figure. At first, I didn't know what it was. The attic is dark and it's hard to see clearly. It looked to be a toy made by someone for their child. I examined it. It wasn't glued or tied together. The sticks were braided into the form of a horse. It was amazing. I decided to have a closer look in the light. Outside in the backyard, I could see how old it was. Then, as I held it up to the sun to get a better look, I accidentally used two hands.

The air around me began to spin. The light became bright and sharp. I could feel the ground under my feet shift and move ever so slightly. My eyes went out of focus. I shut them. When I opened them again, I started to shake. The backyard had changed. Everything that I recognized was gone. In its place was a native village of long ago; wood long houses, fire pits, half-dressed children and natives talking to each other in a language of long, long ago. I was invisible to them. I understood their language and their silent thoughts. The twig horse had brought me back hundreds of years to the time of the ancient Native Americans. Shaking like a leaf, I grabbed the horse again with two hands and came back to my own house and time.

When I realized the power of the twig horse, I vowed to myself to keep it secret. I didn't tell Mom, Dad or Linda. I didn't tell any of my friends. I told no one about the horse and what it could do. I thought no one would believe me anyway. They would think I was the biggest liar in the world or they would call a doctor and have me taken away to the crazy hospital.

In school, I learned dinosaurs roamed through New Jersey tens of thousands of years ago. I began to worry someone would find the horse and be transported back to the time of the dinosaurs. Someone like Linda. I can picture her chasing after one of the smaller dinosaurs trying to pet it then turning in horror as *Tyrannosaurus rex* tries to eat her. I know she would never be able to find her way back. I don't want anyone in my family to find it. They could be gone forever. That's when I taped it to the back of the drawer in my dresser. Now the twig horse is here with me in Pine Ridge. Was it a mistake to bring it here?

I carefully climb out of bed and tiptoe down the hall all the while holding the bag tight to my chest. Standing in the living room doorway, I can make out Vernon on the couch. He's snoring with his back to me.

I enter the kitchen and go out the back door. I listen. No sounds. The black twinkling star sky greets me. The moon is not quite full but manages to light up the backyard. I hear a soft whinny from Red Paint's shed.

I sit back down on the bench and take the horse out of the bag. I'm careful to use just one hand. I slowly unwrap it and stare at it. *How would it be to travel back in time on this land? Would I see Lakota natives and buffalo? Do I want to do this? No, not really. Anything could go wrong. I could end up in the middle of a buffalo stampede. Me invisible. The twig horse trampled to shreds. Gone forever and I stuck forever in a faraway time and place.*

I pick up the tissue paper to rewrap the horse. Something moves on the bench and runs across my arm. A little lizard. I jump up and look down. Oh, no,

I'm holding the twig horse with two hands. I throw it to the ground. Too late.

I know what's going to happen next. I brace myself, grabbing the twig horse up off the ground at the last moment. The air around me fills with wavy lines streaming up from the ground. The light changes and turns bright and sharp. I can feel the wobble of the ground as it moves or shifts slightly under me. As I focus my eyes, I see I'm on the plains but everything is different. The air smells of smoke and cooking meat. Sounds of barking dogs and voices fill the air.

I stand at the edge of a clearing I see water in the distance. I can't see if the water is a lake or a river. In front of me is a native village filled with native houses. The triangle houses are arranged in a circle. They all face one direction. Some of them are decorated with painted designs. I notice even though they are cone shaped, they are not set straight up; they all tilt at an angle. I wonder why. I hold the twig horse very tightly. I can't lose it. It's my only way back.

I move closer to the village. Some native women walk out of the bushes next to the water. It's narrow and flowing down. It's a river. Barefoot and wearing dresses with beaded patterns, the women carry baskets perched on their shoulders. They laugh and talk among themselves. The group breaks up, and each woman heads to a different thípi.

I walk closer to the homes. They can't see or hear me, so I know I'm safe from discovery. A native comes up behind me. He almost bumps into invisible me. I flinch and quickly move to one side. I don't know what would happen if he walked through me. Would it be like a bird flying through a misty cloud? Would I fall? The native man goes into a thípi. The door flaps are open, probably to let some summer air inside.

I peek inside. I'm amazed at all the stuff that's in there. In the center of the space are hot stones. Smoke rises from them. Sticks for firewood are close by. A bag or pouch is hanging over the stones. The smell of meat and onions wafts up from the pouch.

Rolled against the sides are sleeping bags. The walls are covered with all sorts of hanging things: bows and bags holding arrows, shields, a cradleboard to hold a baby and more leather bags. Surprisingly, there are two woven backrests with adjustable sticks for sitting. Wow, the first reclining chairs. The native who entered the thípi relaxes on one of the chairs. There's no one else in the room. Time to move on, I think.

Now that I am inside the village, I look around. Soft gray wisps of smoke curl and rise from the tops of some of the houses. The smell of firewood drifts on the breeze. Native women sit together and, with flat rocks, scrape and pound large sheets of what looks to be leather pegged to the ground; it was probably cut from buffaloes. I hear them whispering together. I move closer to them and realize I can understand their language. They are talking and laughing about someone named Crow.

"Did you see him by the stream?"

"Yes. He stood on the highest rock. He wanted everyone to look at him. Now that he has killed his first buffalo, he thinks he is a great hunter."

"He is a good hunter but he's not humble in front of the other hunters."

"He will learn."

"But it was funny when he slipped on the wet rock and fell into the stream. When he stood up, mud and branches were stuck to his head."

I laugh with the two women but quickly cover my mouth. Then I remember I am a ghost in their world and they can't see or hear me so I let out a big laugh.

Dogs enter the village. They follow a group of native men who carry spears decorated with feathers. A few of them have stick-like harnesses strapped to them with leather strips. The sticks cross in the middle and allow the dogs to pull items loaded onto their dogcarts or *travois*.

The wind gently blows long rectangular strips of meat hanging from what looks to be a clothesline. Small naked boys run around the village with miniature bows and arrows. They yell, laugh, aim, and shoot at each other. Three girls sit on the ground and play with tiny houses and dolls. The littlest one starts to cry when the wind blows her small house across the yard.

No one sees me. I am invisible to everyone. I am Ghost Anna. They call to each other in a different language, but amazingly I can understand what they are saying.

Suddenly, a boy about my age limps by me. I look at his leg.

It's shorter than his other one and he has a twisted ankle, which keeps his foot turned inward. He hurries past me with a firm step and a hop on his bad leg. He glances over his shoulder. An older girl tries to catch up with him.

I hear what they yell to each other.

"White Cloud, stop running away from me. You know I'm right. You can't do this dangerous thing. You will certainly die."

"Bright Star, leave me alone. I can do it and, if I die then I die."

"I will talk to the elders about this and they will stop you," argues Bright Star.

"Talk all you want. They won't listen to you. This is my wish to do this and they will not stop me," retorts White Cloud.

What are they talking about? What is a dangerous thing?

I grab the twig horse with two hands. Immediately I'm back on the bench in my own time. Shaking, I open the back door and slowly pull it toward me, hoping it doesn't squeak. The house is quiet. Vernon is still gently snoring on the couch. In the bedroom, the girls are nestled in the bunk beds under their sheets. I look at Linda in the bottom bunk. She has all her stuffed animals around her. They are a defense against bad dreams.

I put the twig horse on my bed. Where can I hide it? I'm tired and I have no good ideas. Back it goes under the mattress. I'll worry about it tomorrow.

I fall asleep and dream I've become a star in the sky.

Chapter 7

Sacred Pipe – *Čhaŋnúŋpa Wakȟáŋ*

I can barely pick my head up off the pillow. I still feel exhausted after last night. *Serves you right,* I think. *If you're going to be up half the night chasing around after long-dead Lakota people, you deserve to feel groggy and to have a headache.*

I glance over to the bunk beds. Already empty. No surprise there. I'm sure Linda woke up Winnie early so she could get outside to be with Red Paint. Really, someone ought to buy that child a pet of her own.

Noises are coming from the kitchen. I throw my legs over the edge of the bed, stretch, yawn and scratch my head. It's time to face the world. I pad downstairs. Mom is making breakfast. Through the kitchen window, I spy Linda and Winnie holding a bucket for the horse. He gets breakfast too, I guess. I know nothing about caring for a horse. That's OK. Horses are big and scary and not on my to-do list.

"Good morning, Anna. Do you want some eggs for breakfast?" Mom holds the spatula in midair. Mom is distracted. She watches the girls through the window.

Winnie yells, "Whoa, Red Paint."

Mom throws down the spatula and heads out the door. *Trouble on the ranch*, I conclude.

The horse rears up. Winnie pulls on the reins to get him under control. Mom pulls Linda back toward the house away from the horse drama. They stay out there to watch Winnie.

Vernon comes into the kitchen and watches out the window.

"Don't worry about your sister. My Winnie is a natural horsewoman and she'll take good care of her." He pulls two mugs out of the cabinet.

"Do you want some coffee?" he offers.

I can't believe my ears or my good luck. I always want a cup of coffee. It's my dream drink. I just happen to have a set of parents who believe my drink choices should be milk, juice, or water.

"Yes, please. I take it with milk and some sugar." I smile with the lie fresh on my tongue.

"You got it," says Vernon.

I grip the mug. Steaming coffee hits my nose. It smells delicious. I slowly sip it. It is as close to heaven as I imagined. Wonderful coffee. Wonderful Vernon.

"What are you drinking, Anna?" The back door bangs open. Mom looks closely at my mug.

Vernon jumps in. "Oh, don't fret, Maisie, I helped her get her morning joe."

Mom lifts her eyebrows at me and presses her lips together. She doesn't want to make a scene and have Vernon feel bad about giving me coffee.

"Thank you, Vernon." Mom turns her attention back to the stove. "Eggs for everyone?"

I know she'll want to discuss this later. For now, I'm just going to enjoy my first cup of coffee.

"Where's Dad?" I ask.

"He's already down at Oglala Lakota College. He has an early morning meeting with the staff," answers Mom. "Anna, he told me he wants to take you over there to see the school and to show you some of the special rooms they have."

"When will he be back?"

"Anytime now."

I'm not eager to go to the college. I just got out of school and started summer vacation. The last place I want to hang out is at a school. On the other hand, I can't stay here all day with Linda and Winnie. I'm not interested in horses or in playing with little girls. Too bad there aren't some kids my age around here. It suddenly dawns on me this is going to be a very boring vacation.

Back in my room, I really should say "our room", after breakfast, I take the red bag out from under my mattress. It can't stay there. I'm desperate to find a good hiding place. I don't trust Winnie or Linda. They could nose around in my stuff.

I read a mystery book once with this same sort of problem. The story's main character had to hide a famous painting. After eliminating many hiding spots, she decided to hide it in plain sight. She just hung it up on the wall. It worked. Everyone who came into the room assumed it wasn't of any value because it hung in a regular house. They thought it just had to be a copy of a famous painting.

I put the red bag in the plastic bag holding my shampoo and toothpaste. *There*, I thought. *It's just a regular old bag.*

"Anna," calls Dad, "Can you come out here?"

OK, not a fun day ahead. I sigh. "Coming, Dad."

Dad is excitedly telling Vernon and Mom about his morning at the college. "I'm all set up to start classes tomorrow. I'm only doing two and thank goodness they are both scheduled for first and second period. That way I'll have the afternoons to explore the countryside and be with all of you. There's plenty to see around here. Many famous and sacred places to visit."

Oh, wonderful, I think. *No friends, no fun, and field trips to historical sites. The dream of every kid for summer vacation.* I drop my head on my chest.

"Anna, why so glum?" asks Dad, lifting my chin up with his finger.

"I don't know," I whisper.

"Are you still thinking about earning money for a cell phone?" asks Dad, with a smile.

"Yeah, sure." I look up with interest, "But there are no dogs to walk here and I'm not going near the horse."

"I have a proposition for you. You want to earn money and I need some help at the college. I think we could work this out together."

I answer cautiously. "What would I have to do?"

"Oh, that's the fun part," begins Dad.

I think, *Really? Work at the college is 'fun'?*

"You would be my assistant. Not in class but in the Historical Center of the college. They have a wonderful museum with native tools and other things they used long ago. They also have extensive records of Lakota life. I plan on using these resources in my classes. I was hoping you could help me as I gather these up for my lectures. What do you think, Anna?"

Um, not a bad idea. My thoughts jump around in my head. *I'm not doing anything anyway. It could work out. I really want a phone. Maybe I should push for one thing more.* I go for it. "I could take this job but, besides earning money for the phone, I would want you to pay for the monthly charges too. Can you do that?"

Dad looks over at Mom and laughs. "Maybe she'll grow up to be a negotiator."

I don't know what that is but, if it gets me what I want then maybe I will.

"It's a deal," declares Dad. "Let's go to the college and I'll show you around, assistant."

We walk to the college and approach it from the back. It's about a mile from the house. It looks the same as any ordinary stone building, until we walk around to the front. Wow, What a difference. The front is in the shape of a bird. *An eagle,* I think. The walls are painted a terra cotta color with black and white markings. *It's beautiful. I've never seen a building like this.* We go inside. A few people greet my dad. We walk along the hallway to the Historical Center. Inside the room are glass cases containing the Native American objects.

"Let's look at some of these items," says Dad, with a wave of his hand.

The display cases are loaded with all sorts of interesting things. The objects have a small card next to them explaining what they are. I see a buffalo horn spoon; blue-and-red beaded moccasins; a *parfleche,* which is a bag made from animal skin for carrying and storing things; wooden bowls; a woven basket and a red pipe.

"Do you see that red pipe?" Dad points to it. "Pipes have a sacred place in Lakota tradition long ago and today."

I peer at the pipe through the glass. It doesn't seem special.

Dad tells the Lakota story. "Long ago in ancient times when the Lakota and other natives were the only people on the plains, they hunted the buffalo for almost everything they would need in life. It wasn't an easy life. They packed up their belongings, including their houses and moved with the buffalo.

"One year, the Lakota had great difficulty finding enough buffalo for the tribe. The people were hungry and getting sick. The legend goes as such;

Native men went looking for buffalo. They traveled all over and had no luck. A woman dressed in a white buffalo robe approached them. Her name was White Buffalo Calf Woman. She promised to help them. She would bring them a sacred item after four days. She returned on time with a pipe of red stone. The pipe represented the people and all green life on earth. The smoke from the pipe would carry their prayers to the Great Creator, Wakȟáŋ Tȟáŋka. She showed them how to present the pipe to the earth, the sky and the four sacred directions: north, south, east and west. With the pipe, she brought the Seven Sacred Rites of the Lakota. The Lakota prayed with the pipe and the buffalo returned to them. They weren't hungry again."

"Dad, is that story true?" I ask.

"It is an ancient story told from generation to generation. The same as the stories all people pass on to their children. Ancient natives, as people from all ancient cultures—Greeks, Romans, Mayans—wondered about their world and how things came to be as they were. These were the answers they supplied.

"Today, a pipe still functions as the first step in sacred ceremonies. Chief Looking Horse cares for the red pipe today," Dad finishes.

I do have questions for Dad about what I saw when I traveled back in time with the twig horse. I searched for words to ask the questions without giving away my secret.

"Dad, I was reading Winnie's book about our people and I have some questions," I begin.

"That's great, Anna. I didn't think you were interested in native history," enthuses Dad.

"Well, I saw some pictures of a thípi and they were all facing the same way. Why?"

"Anna, the houses are put together facing the east. This helps with the winds which whip across the plains."

"Also, I noticed they were not straight up and down as a cone. Why are they tilted a little?"

"Good observation, Anna. They are tilted a bit. This also helps cut the winds on the plains. It also gives more headroom inside the thípi for taller people. Any other questions?" asks Dad.

"Thanks, not right now," I say. I think *I might have more if I decide to go back but I won't do that. It's too dangerous.*

Chapter 8

Soup - *Waháŋpi*

We all sit down for dinner together tonight. Vernon brings in some extra chairs from the backyard and even Ruby can join us. Vernon cooks another delicious dinner. We eat native fried bread with three sister soup.

Mom is taken with his cooking and recipes. "Now, Vernon, what do you put into this soup? It really is so good."

"Maisie, it's an old special native recipe. Not written down or anything," offers Vernon, winking at Linda.

"Oh, for crying out loud, I've made this soup hundreds of times," pipes up Ruby, while she passes around the basket with the fried bread in it. "And

57

every time I make it, it comes out a little differently. It has three important ingredients: corn, beans, and squash. Then you can add anything else you have in the refrigerator."

Vernon winks at me and turns to Ruby. "Mom, do you know why it's called three sister soup?"

"Humph. Not sure I care," says Ruby.

"Legend, now scientists say the three plants grow well together and help protect each other as they grow," says Vernon, with a decisive nod.

"Oh, enough with old tales," says Ruby. "Pass me some more soup." Everyone laughs.

After the cleanup, we all sit outside under the stars. I'm getting to enjoy this. At home, we're all so busy. After dinner, Dad retreats to the study to work on the store's accounts. Mom sits at the dining-room table reading through seed and plant catalogs deciding which ones she'll order for Čhetáŋ's Nursery. I go upstairs to do my homework. And Linda watches kid shows on TV. I know it's silly to think it's a big thing to just sit outside and look at the stars but it feels nice to be all together doing the same thing.

Dad breaks the quiet. "While we're staying out here, we should visit some of the important parks and natural wonders. This land is so different from New Jersey. We should explore it."

"You should," agrees Vernon. "It's Lakota land and the girls should learn about it. The land, the air, the waters, the living creatures belong to all of us to care for; even though you live far away, you are part of all of this." He waves his hand to indicate the stars and all we see before us.

Only I hear Dad whisper, "Bridge the Divide."

"Where are you thinking of going?" asks Mom.

"I am thinking about Devils Tower. The park is not far from here," answers Dad.

"Girls, that's a sacred place for all of us," says Vernon. "It's where the White Buffalo Calf Woman brought the pipe to us."

I speak up. "The pipe that helped bring the buffalo back?"

Vernon looks surprised. "You know that story?"

I smile at Dad, who looks proud of me. "Yes, I'm learning."

Linda lifts her head up from a string bracelet she's weaving with directions from Winnie. "What kind of tower did you say?"

Winnie, still working the threads on the bracelet, answers, "Devils Tower."

"No, no, no, I'm not going," yells Linda. "That's not a good place." She's about to cry.

Mom comforts her with, "Shh, shh, Linda. It's not a bad place. It's a sacred place for native people."

"Then why is it called the 'Devil'? asks Linda

"Actually, that's not its real name," explains Dad. "That's the name the government gave it. Its native name is Bear Lodge, *Matȟó Thípila*. The Lakota are working to have the name changed."

Linda is relieved. "Are there bear cubs there?"

"The tower is huge. It's made of rock and rises out of the ground. It is over twelve hundred feet high," begins Mom in her storyteller's voice. She loves to share native stories and calls them "rich".

"Many, many years ago, the tribes would travel through the plains and the Black Hills to collect berries and herbs. Everyone would go: women, babies, children, warriors. It was time to be together.

"One day, as they were camping, three girls, good friends, wandered off together. They soon realized they were lost. They called out to their mothers. They heard nothing; however, bears heard their cries and lumbered toward them. The girls screamed and ran but they knew it was hopeless. They could never outrun the bears.

"A voice called out to them, 'Climb the hill. *Pahá kiŋ alí po,*'"

The girls ran to a small hill in their pathway. They stood on top of the hill, wondering how this small hill would keep the bears from eating them. The hill began to shake and move. Up and up and up it rose out of the ground. The girls clung together on the top. They saw they were on top of a rock mountain. They were safe from the bears.

"The angry and frustrated bears would not give up. They tried to scale the rock tower. Digging their claws into the side of the rock, they left long marks on the side of the rock tower. They could not reach the girls. Rocks fell from the sides and killed the bears.

"But now the girls were stuck on the rock tower. How could they get down? Large birds appeared in the sky and flew toward the girls. Each girl was picked up by a bird and carried off the top of the tower. The girls were deposited safely on the ground and were gathered up in the arms of their frightened mothers."

"I think the name of the tower should be 'Brave Lakota Girl Rock,'" announces Linda. "Are we going there tomorrow?"

Dad laughs. Linda always wants to do everything right away.

"Not tomorrow but soon," promises Dad, as he stretches. "It's been a long day. I'm off to bed."

"Me too," says Mom.

Everyone agrees and goes in for the night.

I hear Dad calling my name from the hall. "Anna?"

"What, Dad?" I call back.

"I'd like you to come to the college with me tomorrow morning. I have some things I'll need from the Historical Center. You can start earning your phone money," he says.

"OK by me," I say.

"See you bright and early," ends Dad.

I lie in bed thinking of everything that has happened since I've arrived at Pine Ridge. *It's not going to be such a terrible summer after all. Vernon and Ruby are nice to everyone. The food is really good. Linda is occupied with Winnie and the horse, so she's not bugging me to play with her and I'm going to earn money for my cell phone. I don't mind not doing the dog walking. Who wants to walk past Jason's house every day? Only Liz. No, it's turning out to be a pretty good summer, after all.*

I hear soft breathing from Linda and Winnie. I stare up at the ceiling. When I see the wooden beam, the twig horse pops into my mind. *What am I going to do about it? Just because I used it once doesn't mean I have to do it again. I do know that it still works. So what? I always knew that. That's why I hid it so carefully and why I worry about someone discovering it. It's never going to lose its powers.*

I turn over in the bed and face the wall. Pulling the sheet up to my neck, I close my eyes. *Go to sleep*, I tell myself. My eyes blink open. The scene with Bright Star and White Cloud replays as a movie before me.

Bright Star was angry at White Cloud but it was more than that. She didn't want him to do something because she was afraid of what would happen to him. White Cloud was defiant but when he announced to her he didn't care if he died, she looked as if she were going to cry.

What terribly dangerous thing is he going to do? I'll never know the answer. Unless...I go back.

Chapter 9

Hunt – *Wakhúwa*

No coffee this morning. Mom already set the table. At my seat, there's a big glass of orange juice. Dad is at the stove trying to flip pancakes in the pan.

"Whoa," he yells at the pancake. It has slipped sideways and is hanging off the side of the pan.

I play a game in my head. Score: pancake, one; Dad, zero. He tries again, holding the spatula like a native war stick. This time the pancake falls onto the gas flames with a sizzle. Score: pancake, two; Dad, zero.

"What are you doing, Oren?" demands Mom. "You're making a mess all over the stove. We can't eat those pancakes. They're burned."

"I'm just practicing my cooking technique." Dad gives it another try. He pours more batter onto the pan.

Mom swoops in and grabs the spatula. "We need pancakes now. Practice another time."

Dad laughs and shrugs. "That's one way to get out of cooking. Be bad at it."

At home, Mom and Dad take turns cooking breakfast and dinner. He does OK at home. I think he just doesn't want to today.

"Anna, we'll leave for the college right after breakfast. My class is at 9 o'clock."

"OK," I say.

Linda and Winnie come in from the backyard and sit at the table.

"Girls, wash your hands," instructs Mom.

"Mom, today Winnie and I are going to clean out Red Paint's shed and exercise him and brush him and…," says Linda shoving pancake and drippy syrup in her mouth.

"Linda, please don't talk with your mouth full," reminds Mom. "I guess you're going to have a busy day."

Linda nods her head. Her mouth is too full to answer. I'm glad I'm leaving for the morning. I need a break from the girls.

Ruby makes her way into the kitchen. She pushes the walker slowly and takes small sliding steps. "What's this I hear about Red Paint?"

"Grandma, we're taking care of him today," says Winnie.

"I'm glad to hear this. It's been a while since the shed's been cleaned out. He's your responsibility, Winnie," reminds Ruby.

"I know. We're on it."

I'd rather scrub floors at the Historical Center than take care of that horse. I'm glad the girls are happy to do it.

The college is not far from the Sandozes' house. I follow Dad into the center. He heads for the back room where all the records are kept and stops in front of a file cabinet labeled Lakota History.

"Anna, there are written first-hand accounts of where the Lakota came from before they moved to this area. I want you to find them and pull out those papers for me. The accounts are stored in order by years. Do you think you can do this?" asks Dad.

To get my own phone? No problem. I answer with confidence, "Absolutely."

"OK," I say.

"Get to work. I'll be in classroom number 114 for two class periods. I'll meet you back here for lunch."

He pats my shoulder and leaves.

OK, I think. *Get to work.*

The file drawers are sticky to open. Dust covers most of the metal cabinets. I conclude they haven't been opened for a while. My imagination runs wild and I picture the cabinets sealed shut during the last buffalo stampede.

A chief yells, "We have to shut the cabinets and save the papers from buffalo hooves."

I imagine I'm a Lakota princess. *"I'll save the papers."*

The chief says, "Good. Ride this horse to the center."

My imaginary bubble pops. I'm not getting on a horse to save anything. Even in my imagination. I work my way through several file folders. I find nothing on when the Lakota first came to this land. *This is going to be harder than I thought.*

I watch the clock on the wall. It's a long time until lunch. I wonder if I have time to go back to Vernon's house for a bit. I could check on the girls. *Anna, stop lying to yourself. You want to get the twig horse and check on White Cloud.* I argue with myself. *I just want to make sure he's OK. What business is that of yours?* It's as if there are two Annas in my head.

I tell myself, *It's no big deal.* I'll be back before lunch and I'll have time to find those papers for Dad. I gallop down the road like horses are chasing me. I slip into the house unseen. The windows are open and I can hear Linda, Winnie and Mom outside in the yard.

Mom says, "I'm walking to the grocery store. When you girls finish up here, wash up. Your lunches and Ruby's are in the refrigerator."

I stand very still in the bedroom. The door bangs shut. Mom must be gone. I pick up the red bag and leave as quietly as I can. Holding the bag tightly, I walk toward the college but stop halfway. There's a lone tree on the side of the road. I duck behind it. Taking the twig horse out of the bag, I place the bag at the bottom of the tree. Here I go. I stand still and grab the horse with two hands. The wavy lines appear in the air. The dust and sand of the land make tiny tornadoes around me. The light is blinding. The noise is deafening. Wait. What "noise?"

I quickly look around for the source of the thunderous noise. Oh, no, not far away hundreds of buffalo hooves are moving in this direction straight toward invisible me. Can an invisible person still be trampled to death? I'm not waiting around to see what happens.

I start to run as fast as I can. I'm running up a hill. I just keep going. The buffalo are behind me. I also hear people screaming. Everything is getting closer to me. I'm breathing hard. I must work harder in PE next year. My lungs don't seem very strong. I give a quick glance behind me. Now I see the people. They are waving blankets and screaming at the buffalo. They are herding them up this hill, too.

Quickly, I change direction. I turn away from the hill and the commotion behind me. The buffalo stampede up the hill. Then a very strange thing happens. The buffalo disappear. They just vanish from sight. Where are they? I notice the natives chasing them are mostly women and children. Where are the men? They all stop at the top of the hill and look down. I hear animals moaning and whoops of natives.

I make my way up the hill and stand with the natives gazing down. I, too, look down. The buffalo are being speared by the men. The fall from the hill has landed the animals into a steep canyon where many of them have died.

I think it's a good thing Linda is not here to see this. She'd be running down the canyon wall to try to save the buffalo. I remember what Dad told us about the buffalo and the Lakota people and how they thanked the Creator for the gift of the buffalo. They couldn't live without it. Linda is too young to understand that.

It's time to return to Pine Ridge. I spot the lone tree where I stood with the twig horse. There it is on the ground. I grab hold of it with two hands, close my eyes, and feel myself moving ahead in time and space.

I quickly put the twig horse back in the bag and pull the tie shut with my teeth. I run as fast as I can to the college. *What time is it?* I wonder. *I don't know how long I've been gone. Maybe Dad has come looking for me. I'll be in trouble.* I'm out of breath, again, as I go down the hall to the file room. Oh, no, I hear footsteps behind me. I can't stop to look.

With long strides, I reach the room and hurry inside. I pull open a file drawer, grab a file, and sit down at the desk in the room. I have to slow my breathing. I sound as if I've just run a marathon. Someone enters the room. I try to casually look up as if it doesn't matter to me who comes in but it's not Dad. An older lady carrying a file smiles at me and replaces the file in a drawer. Whew, I made it.

I decide to get to work. I pore over papers and documents about the Oglala Lakota. I find an interesting account of a "buffalo jump". It explains exactly what I just saw: how the natives make a ruckus to drive the buffalo over a canyon wall. It says it was an efficient way to hunt the bison.

The only difficulty with it was the serious injuries to the people. It explained the buffalo are impossible to herd as a group. When they run together, some turn left, some turn right, and some even decide to reverse direction. In that case, the buffalo would head right toward the women and children chasing them. The people would be knocked down and run over. Some would die.

I'm glad the Lakota no longer have to hunt the buffalo.

Dad taps me on the shoulder. "I see you're working hard, Anna." He smiles.

I feel guilty. "Dad, I haven't found what you want yet but I'm not giving up."

"That's my girl."

We walk home for lunch. Upon opening the front door, the sound of children's cries greets us.

Ruby sits on the sofa and faces a sobbing Linda and Winnie.

"Do you girls, understand what you did?"

They're crying too hard to do anything but nod their heads up and down.

What's going on now?

Chapter 10

Trickster – *Wičhágnayes'a*

Dad walks over to the girls and points to the twig chairs. "Both of you sit down and tell me what this is all about."

Linda blurts out, "Red Paint is gone and it's our fault." She starts wailing louder than ever.

Dad turns to Winnie. "Why is Red Paint gone?"

"We left the gate open and he ran away. We looked all over for him. He's just gone." She wipes her nose with her arm.

Ruby shakes her finger at the girls. "I warned them but they didn't listen."

Dad sighs. "This can be fixed. Let's go. We'll take Vernon's truck and find the horse."

We all march out of the house. Dad backs up the truck and asks Winnie, "Which way do you think he would go?"

I can tell Winnie is too upset to think straight. "Let's head right, away from the college, and look on the grasslands. If he's not there then we can go in the other direction," I say

"All right. Everyone, keep your eyes open," requests Dad.

We drive a few miles up the road and see nothing. They whip their heads from left to right, staring as hard as they can. I look down and notice they are holding hands. I'm glad they have become such good friends.

After going many miles up the road, Dad decides to turn the truck around and go back. "We'll see if he ran the other way."

We drive and drive. No Red Paint. Winnie is anxious. She's biting her nail and jiggling her leg.

"Where is he?" she wails. "If he went running in the Badlands, he could have fallen off a cliff and be really hurt."

"Let's head back home. Winnie, your Dad can take the car and look with us," Dad says decisively. We pull onto the gravel driveway. Winnie opens the truck's door before Dad even stops the engine. She bolts into the house.

"Let's just wait here," says Dad.

Suddenly Winnie is at the door yelling, "Everyone, come here. Hurry,"

We all file out of the truck. Linda runs into the house.

Vernon greets us with a big smile. "It's all right."

Out the kitchen window, we see Winnie and Linda hugging and kissing Red Paint. We all feel relief.

"What happened, Vernon?" asks Dad.

"When I came home my mom told me the whole story," he explains. "I thought the horse might wander away if given a chance but I also knew he'd be back for his oat dinner and, sure enough, he strolled into the backyard as if he had just been out for a little walk. He went to the shed for his dinner. Horses are a lot smarter than we think."

I watch as Winnie fastens the back gate securely. She and Linda come into the house.

Ruby calls to them, "Come here, girls. I want to ask you something."

The girls sit down on the twig chairs. I stand in the doorway to hear what Ruby will say.

"Did both of you make a plan and a promise to take care of Red Paint today?" she asks.

They nod their heads.

"What happened to Red Paint? Tell us."

Winnie starts, "We planned to exercise him, brush him and clean out his shed. We did the exercising and brushing but it got hot so we thought we would wait until it got cooler to do the shed. "

Linda picks up the story. "Winnie knows where some chokeberries are. We thought it would be fun to pick some while we were waiting for it to get cool."

"We were picking the berries and eating some then we remembered we still had to clean out the shed. When we got back to the house, we saw the gate was open and Red Paint was gone," explains Winnie. "We're so sorry. Aren't we, Linda?"

Linda nods her head. "We'll never leave the gate open again."

Ruby gives the girls a stern look. "This is not about leaving the gate open, though you should always close it behind you. It's about finishing the work you promised to do before you go off to do something else.

"We Lakota, have a legend about the Trickster. You didn't meet him this time but he's around and he tricks people into making them do the wrong things. He could have easily tricked both of you.

"One day, long ago, two sisters were playing with their small toy thípi."

I think, *Really, When I was in the native village the first time, I saw some girls playing that way.*

Ruby continues, "Their mother wanted to do some weaving with the other women. She asked them if they would stop playing and, instead, watch over their small brother. They promised their mother they would play with their brother and make sure he would be safe. Their mother trusted the words of the girls.

"They did play a game called 'find me' with the boy. They all had fun hiding under the blankets in the thipi and behind other village houses. The children laughed and ran through the camp and the girls were true to their word. They stayed close to their little brother.

"Then, the Trickster appeared. He told the sisters he saw big juicy chokeberries in the grass by the river.

"The sisters told him to go away. They were watching their brother for their mother. When their mother came back they would go down by the river to get the chokeberries.

"Ah, but the Trickster was as cunning as a fox. He told them he saw other girls down by the river gathering chokeberries and there would be none left for them.

"And he added, 'Won't your mother be happy to have berries to eat? Won't she hug you and tell you, you were her very clever girls to find such delicious chokeberries?'

"They told him they couldn't go. They had to watch their brother.

"That didn't stop the Trickster. He promised he would take very good care of the boy until they came back with their baskets filled to the top with the best berries in the world.

"Those silly girls looked at each other and said 'yes' to the Trickster. Off they ran, down to the river, holding hands and laughing the whole way.

"They did find lots of berries. They gathered and ate to their hearts' content. They returned to the village full and happy. Their mother stood outside their thípi with her arms crossed on her chest.

"'Where have you been?' she asked, as she looked at the girls.

"They held out their full baskets with big smiles. Here, Mother, all for you.'

"She knocked the baskets to the ground. The girls were shocked. What was wrong with their mother? Didn't she realize they got all the berries as a surprise for her?

"'Where is your little brother?' she screamed.

"'A man is watching him for us. He must be in the thípi,' said one of the girls. They all hurried inside to look. No man and no baby brother.

"The mother and the girls began to howl and tear at their clothes. Men and women ran to them to find out what was wrong.

"One of the last women to arrive carried a heavy blanket. She stopped before the mother and handed the bundle to her. Inside was the small brother, sound asleep.

"The woman said, I saw the Trickster talking to the sisters. I knew he was planning trouble. When I saw the girls leave their brother with him, I grabbed the boy and ran away.'

"The mother hugged the woman. She hugged her daughters. She held her small son tightly in her arms."

Ruby pauses and concludes, "Without the woman's sharp eyes, the Trickster could have run away with the boy. They might never have seen him again. Girls, what did the sisters do wrong?"

"They should have kept their promise to their mom," answers Linda.

"They shouldn't listen to what other people say. They should think and do what they know is right," replies Winnie.

Linda gives a huge grin. "Thank goodness the Trickster didn't come here. We might have been tricked."

Winnie sighs. "Linda, it's sorta as if he did come here. We walked away from our promises and lost Red Paint for a while and got everyone upset."

"Oh," says Linda. She wrinkles her forehead as she tries to understand.

Save me from little sisters. It takes a long time for them to catch on to things.

"Well, girls, I told you about the Trickster because we can all learn lessons from him," says Ruby. "Now, what's for dinner, Vernon?"

I think a nice cold glass of iced coffee would help settle my nerves.

Chapter 11

Older Sister to a Boy – *Thaŋké*

The next morning dawns bright, sunny and beautiful. At breakfast, Dad announces the college is closed for the day. It's administration day. Whatever that is? Well, for me, it means I won't be going to the college records room.

"I think we should do something today," says Mom as she pours cereal into bowls. "How about we go to a historic site?"

I groan inside my head. *I don't mind seeing new things or historical places but all of us will travel together. Sometimes Linda and Winnie are calm and quiet and many times, they whine, complain and are generally grumpy.*

"Winnie and I are planning to go to the youth center pool," whines Linda. "We've been waiting to go for a long time."

OK here we go. Problem City. We haven't even had a spoonful of cereal yet, I think.

"Oren, what do you think?" asks Mom. She shakes the last of the flakes out of the box.

I hope that's not going into my bowl. I hate the crumbs in the bottom of the cereal box. They get all mushy in the milk, I think.

"I think we can do both things, Maisie. The pool in the morning and a trip in the afternoon. How about that?" says Dad. He looks around the table as Linda claps her hands.

"OK. We're decided," agrees Mom. She passes out the bowls of cereal.

Which one do I get? The one with bottom-dwelling flakes. I dip my spoon into the cereal and come up with a pile of stuck together mush floating in milk. A great start to the day.

"Mom, do I have to go to the pool with the girls?" I ask. A plan starts forming in my head.

"Anna, what do you want to do?" asks Dad. He crunches on the good flakes.

"I want to spend some time reading about Lakota life. Vernon has some good books here at the house," I say. I put a very sincere look on my face.

"Oh, OK. We'll go to the pool and then come back here for lunch," agrees Dad. "This afternoon we'll head out to Devils Tower." He shifts his eyes to Linda, who's not paying attention. She's trying to get all the raisins onto her spoon.

It takes a while for them to get pool-ready, but soon quiet fills the house. Just Ruby and I are left. I hear her TV on in her room.

I know I shouldn't lie to my parents but *how on earth can I explain I will use a twig horse and go back in time to be with ancient Lakota people? It can't be done. After we leave Pine Ridge, I won't lie to them again. I promise myself. I just want to find out how White Cloud and Bright Star are doing. Is the dangerous thing resolved yet?*

I won't have much time to do this. Just a few hours. I take the twig horse outside and stand by the bench. In a matter of seconds, I am back in the time of the ancient Lakota. Ghost Anna is back. I decide to wander around the campsite. The sun is shining here too. The cooking pots simmer with good smells. The children play a chasing game with each other and familiar voices argue. Following the sound, I soon come upon White Cloud and Bright Star.

White Cloud whittles a stick. *Is it a spear or an arrow?* I can't tell. Bright Star uses a smooth rock to pound round red berries in a wooden bowl. Both talk to each other without looking up from their task. They talk softly.

"Bright Star, I know you are worried about me. Please, don't be. I would never do anything foolish that would cause harm to you or to me," says White Cloud. He rubs the stick with a rock to remove the bark.

"White Cloud, I know you will try to keep safe, but you have a bad leg and crooked foot; you have those because of me."

What? His bad leg is Bright Star's fault?

"Sister, that happened so long ago. It was my fault, not yours," says White Cloud.

Bright Star shakes her head. "I should have stayed home with you that day. I could hear the woman yelling to chase the buffalo off the cliff. I wanted to see the buffalo jump. So, I took you with me. You were heavy to carry. I asked you to walk with me.

"I didn't see some of the buffalo change direction and come toward us. It happened so fast. You were knocked to the ground and your poor leg was trampled.

"I scooped you up. Blood was pouring from your leg. I ran back to the village for help. The medicine woman put sacred grass and herbs on you and bound up your poor foot. When I asked her if you would be all right, she shook her head."

"Sister, look at me. I am all right," replies White Cloud.

They both fall silent and continue working. I watch them as they whittle and pound. Accidents happen. His sister didn't mean for him to get hurt but he did. I still don't know what he wants to do that she thinks is so dangerous. I wish he would think about it because I can hear his thoughts.

I sit down on the ground with them. A dog wanders by, stops, and stares at me. Animals have special sight powers. The dog can see me. I hope they don't notice the dog watching me.

"Shoo, go away," I whisper. He cocks his ears and moves off to something more interesting. It's happening. White Cloud talks to himself in his head. I hear him say, *I will go on the Vision Quest. It's something I must do because of my leg. My sister will not stop me.*" He throws the stone to the ground, takes the stick and heads toward their thípi.

It's time for me to return to my world. As I turn to go, a native man runs into the campsite. He hollers and yells. He waves his arms and calls all the people to come. *Now, what is this?* I wonder.

The Lakota hurry to follow behind him. They are all so noisy. I can't understand what they are saying. I decide I still have some time before the family returns from the pool. I follow the crowd.

We run and fast walk toward the hills of the Badlands. Before we reach them, the native stops and points to the ground. The tribe becomes silent. They all stare at something I can't see because I'm in the back of the crowd. Invisible me walks to the front where the man is.

There it is. A dead horse. They point and talk and then step back.

"What is it?" someone asks.

That's when a light bulb goes on in my head. Anna, you never saw one horse in camp. They didn't use horses to chase the buffalo either. They don't have any horses.

Someone calls out, "It's a big dog. It has four legs and a tail. It's a big dog." The people turn to one another and repeat the words "big dog". They are happy to give this strange creature a name. They gather around it and grab hold of its legs. The horse is dragged into the camp.

It's time for me to go. I have a lot to think about. I arrive back minutes before the pool crowd. They look happy, warm, and wet.

Mom says, "Let's get out of the bathing suits. I have lunch ready in the refrigerator."

"Can Ruby come to the tower with us?" asks Linda. She throws her wet towel on the floor.

"I'm afraid not, honey," answers Mom. "The doctor is stopping by to check on her this afternoon. I think one of her friends is coming to visit, too.

"Pick up the towel, Linda," adds Mom.

"How was your morning, Anna?" asks Dad.

"I learned a lot about our people but I still have questions," I answer truthfully, thinking about all I've seen today.

"We can talk later," says Dad.

After lunch, we pile into the car and head to Bear Lodge, also called Devils Tower. I like the name Bear Lodge better.

As we drive, I rest my head and pretend I've fallen asleep.

I want to think about what I've seen and heard this morning.

I know White Cloud wants to do a Vision Quest. I don't know what that is or why Bright Star says it's dangerous. I am surprised to find out the Lakota had never seen a horse before. Natives chasing buffalo on horses are in history books, on TV and in movies. Why don't they have any? Questions pile up for Dad.

The car pulls into the parking lot. We all stare up at the tower. It's huge and dark. It stands all by itself in the open space. Long dark scrape marks in the sides start at the top and continue downward. It's surrounded by pine trees, boulders, and small trees clinging to the bottom of the black and gray tower-rock. There's a walking path all around it.

"Who's ready for a hike?" asks Mom.

"I am," yells Linda. She turns to Winnie. "Let's look for baby bears." She starts to lead the way. We all follow.

Mom orders, "Stay together, please."

The path is well worn and gravelly. We pass other families on the way.

"Get a look at that view." Dad points to a valley in the distance.

Winnie wonders aloud. "Do you think the Lakota girls came from that valley, Oren?"

Dad chuckles. "I guess so. The legend is very old. Who knows how the land looked back then? Maybe there was a river there."

As we make our way around the tower, I notice colorful pieces of cloth tied to the trees closest to the huge rock. Linda goes to touch one of them.

"No, Linda," warns Mom. "Those are special prayer cloths the Lakota have tied to the trees. This place is sacred, and when the people come here, they offer up their prayers and wishes to the great Creator. We mustn't touch the cloths."

Linda shrugs and hurries ahead of us. She rounds a corner and is soon out of sight. The sound of her sneakers crunching on the gravel disappears.

The brush is thicker, and the tower seems taller on the other side of it. There are many more boulders on the ground. Dad points to the empty spots on the rock where the boulders used to be.

"Linda," Mom calls. She is nowhere in sight. "Oren, did you see which way she went?"

"No, I didn't." Dad walks faster. "I'm sure she's just around this bend."

"Linda," we all call. There's no sign of her.

Where, oh, where is Linda?

Chapter 12

Bear – *Matȟó*

"Oren, you don't think she slipped and is in the ravine?" asks a nervous Mom. She walks to the side of the path and looks down.

"Listen, I'll head back and look along the path. Maisie, you and the girls go ahead. Call her name as you search."

Quickly we move around the tower calling Linda's name. Some concerned hikers hear us and stop to ask if they can help.

"Yes, please," says Mom. "She's a little girl with dark hair and red shorts on."

The name "Linda" echoes and repeats again. I stop to listen. Do I hear her calling to us? In the distance, I hear a faint call, "Help."

"Mom, do you hear that?" I ask.

She stops and stands silently.

"He-e-l-l-l-p-p."

"Yes, that's her," says Mom.

Winnie, Mom and I move swiftly toward the sound. Closer and closer we get to the side of the tower. We clearly see a black hole in the rocky side but no Linda. Dad is closing in behind us. He's out of breath from running.

"Is she in there?" He points at the dark cave. "Linda."

"Help me" comes from the mouth of the cave.

"Coming, sweetheart." Dad begins the climb up. "Are you hurt?"

"No. I'm stuck."

"Be careful, Oren," says Mom. "Maybe we should get a park ranger."

Dad runs quickly to the cave and disappears inside. We watch him walk out holding a dirty but happy Linda. "Her sneaker was stuck between two rocks," he explains.

"Hi, guys," she calls. She waves to us as if she were the queen and we're the lowly peasants. Little sisters, all the drama,

Mom grabs her, shakes her and hugs her. "What did I tell you about staying together? No wandering away."

"Mom, this was important. I thought I heard a baby bear crying in the cave. I went inside to help him; but guess what? There's a hole in the cave wall and the wind comes through it and makes a crying sound," explains Linda.

"Just stay by us," orders Mom.

We continue the walk around the tower and head back to the parking lot.

We return to the house at dinnertime. Vernon is home from work and bustles around the kitchen. The smell of burgers makes my mouth water. Vernon sets a platter of burgers in buns on the table. He pulls roasted corn on the cob off the outside grill. The corn joins the burgers.

"Vernon, you should open a restaurant," declares Dad, chomping down on the bun. "Everything you make is excellent."

After our trip to the tower and long walk around it, I am starving. "I could eat a bear." I take a big bite of my burger.

Vernon throws back his head and laughs. "Actually, you are eating something as big as a bear."

I stop chewing and look at Vernon. With my mouth full and my words garbled I manage to ask, "What do you mean?

"Tonight, we eat Lakota food. Buffalo. Juicy, huh?" he says.

I finish chewing and swallow quickly. "Really?" I don't know what else to say.

Mom smacks her lips and says, "Delicious." Dad agrees with her. Linda puts the burger down and picks up the corn. I decide it's not bad. I eat the Lakota way.

After dinner, Dad stays at the table to work on his lesson plans for the next day. Everyone else goes into the front room to watch a contestant show called *Singing with the Stars*.

"Dad, can I ask you questions about the Lakota?"

"Sure, Anna, I'm done here." He closes his laptop.

I can't tell Dad that my questions concern what I saw when I went back in time. I promise myself that, after this trip, I will never lie again. "Dad, I read that the Lakota didn't always have horses. Where did the horses come from and when did they find them?"

"The Spanish ranchers who came to settle in the New World brought the horses with them in the 1500s. They lived in Mexico and Texas. Horses would escape from the ranches and run free. Some others would be stolen by native tribes and brought to places further north. By about 1750 the first horses were seen on the plains. The plains Indians quickly saw how helpful horses could be for them.

"Up until then, native women and dogs dragged all the houses and supplies. They were challenged when dragging the poles necessary for setting up the thípi. The poles are long and heavy. The buffalo hide made heavy bundles to transport. Horses were and are seen as sacred and special.

"If they didn't have horses, how did they find and hunt the buffalo?"

Dad shakes his head. "It was the most difficult task. Imagine a tribe of men, women, children and babies walking miles and miles following scouts who think they've seen a herd.

"They would sneak up on the bison with bows, arrows, and spears to kill them. It didn't always work. Many people were hurt or killed by stampeding buffalo. In fact, the ancient Lakota tribe had periods of starvation whenever the buffalo were hard to locate.

"Herding buffalo is similar to catching birds. They go in all directions. When they had the horses, they became excellent riders and hunters."

"Thanks, Dad. You're a good teacher," I say.

My thoughts are running as wild horses through my head. *Today, I saw the tribe discover the first horse. I should feel glad for them but the horse was dead. How can one dead horse help them hunt buffalo? I wonder, whether there are other horses, live ones, of course, on the plains where the encampment is? Can any of the tribe find them? The bigger question is whether they would even know what to do with horses if they found them.*

Dad and I hear lots of noise coming from the front room. The TV is off, and the loud voices are coming toward the kitchen. They are all singing off-key. My family has a few talents but singing is not one of them. They are in a conga line holding on to each other's shoulders.

They sing, "I scream, you scream, we all scream for ice cream," It's loud, to the point, and effective.

Dad laughs and scoops his papers off the table. "All right, all right, I surrender the kitchen to you. Have your frozen treat,"

I am disappointed that I didn't get to ask Dad about the Vision Quest. I will try tomorrow. Right now, Mom has the chocolate marshmallow ice cream on the table.

"Anna, how many scoops do you want?" she asks.

Does she really have to ask me? I'm an ice cream freak. If left alone with the tub, I could do lots of damage to it. Yum.

Chapter 13

Seek – *Olé*

In the morning, I'm back at the college with Dad. I pretend I'm a prisoner locked in the records room. Walking back and forth in front of the file cabinets, I wring my hands and moan, "There is no one here to help me escape. What am I going to do?"

I notice the small window up by the ceiling. "I can do it. I'll climb out of the window." I drag the chair over and climb up.

With that, the door opens, and a man comes in. He looks startled to see me. He asks, "Can I help you?"

I'm totally embarrassed. I spit out a lie: "I was just checking the window to see if it opened. It's a little hot in here." I jump down.

"Well, you probably didn't know this but this room is air-conditioned." He points to the thermostat on the wall, "Just turn it down."

"Oh, thank you."

When he leaves, I get back to work. Enough imagination. As I search for files on Lakota migration, I come across a drawer marked "Lakota Ceremonies." Curious to see if any of the ceremonies mention a Vision Quest, I flip through the pages and there it is. The words jump out at me: "Vision Quest." The excitement fills me. I can't believe my good luck.

I begin to read:

A Vision Quest can be taken by anyone who seeks spiritual guidance from the Creator. The seeker goes to a Holy Man, *Wičháša Wakȟáŋ*, for advice and guidance. Following a ceremony in the sweat lodge, the individual on the quest goes to an isolated place for four days without food or water, waiting for a personal vision. When a vision does happen, the seeker returns to the Holy Man and has him interpret the vision for him.

Oh, wow, no wonder Bright Star does not want White Cloud to do this quest. He would be all alone and without help, if something went wrong. He could trip and fall down a hill or be attacked by a wild animal or hurt his foot again and be unable to walk.

I put the file down. She's right. This is not for him. Somehow, I must prevent this from happening. I have no clue how but I do sense danger for White Cloud. If I can't find a way to stop him, I don't know what I'll do. There has to be something.

Dad knocks at the open door. "Anna, are you just about done?"

"Yes, Dad and look what I found," I hold up a file, I just pulled from the drawer. It has the words "Lakota Migration" on the tab.

"Great job," says Dad as he reaches for the file. "It's just what I need for my next lesson. I'm proud of you, Anna. You've taken on this job and you're doing well."

OK, now the guilt washes over me like water off a cliff. I'm trying to help Dad but I'm really trying to help a native boy, alive hundreds of years ago.

Wait, Anna, I tell myself. *I'm not going to feel bad. I'm "Bridging the Divide." Isn't that what Dad wants? White Cloud's time to my time. I shouldn't feel bad at all.*

"Let's go home and see what everyone is doing," suggests Dad. "We're done here for today."

On the way home, I ask Dad about sweat lodges.

"Anna, they've always been an important part of native ceremonies. The lodge is built with willow trees and hides. It's completely dark inside. People use heat, steam, prayers and the pipe to renew their spirits inside the lodge. Does that help?"

"Thanks, Dad," I answer. "Have you ever been in a sweat lodge?"

"Yes, I have. It was a sacred experience, one I'll never forget," says Dad.

When we're in the house, we hear loud voices, laughing and drumming coming from Ruby's room. Everyone is squeezed into the bedroom. Ruby, Mom, and Vernon perch on the bed. Vernon beats on a small drum. Linda and Winnie jump around the room and wave parts of Native American costumes in the air.

Dad and I poke our heads into the room. "What is all this?" asks Dad. He holds up a dress covered from top to bottom with cone-shaped jingle bells.

"We're getting ready," announces Winnie.

"Ready for what?" I ask.

"There's going to be a powwow here in Pine Ridge," says an excited Linda. She hops from foot to foot. "And we're invited to go. Winnie, can we bring Red Paint?"

Winnie smiles. "Sorry, Linda. Lots of people will be there. There's no room for a horse."

"Oh, that's too bad," answers Linda. "What will we do there, anyway?"

"Well, first comes the parade. Our Lakota tribe will all be dressed in their best ceremonial clothes. The chiefs and some of the men will wear deerskin pants with fringe and shirts covered with beads, designs, and feathers. On their heads, you will see headdresses with beads and eagle feathers. They look to be the famous chiefs of long ago.

"The women and children are in the parade too. The women and girls wear beautiful dresses also decorated with beads.

"After the parade, the fun begins. We have contests and games and lots of food."

Linda sighs. "I wish it were today."

Ruby holds up the jingle dress. "Our Winnie will be the best dancer in her Lakota dress." She takes a blue fringed shawl from the pile of clothes on her bed. "This is your mother's, Winnie. You're big enough now to dance with it."

"My mother must have looked beautiful dancing with this."

"That she did. The most beautiful woman in Pine Ridge," says Vernon.

"The powwow is next weekend. We need to decide what we'll do this afternoon," says Mom. "Any ideas?"

"There's a student art show at the college. They have sculptures, paintings, photos, and other things there. I thought we could walk down and look," suggests Dad. "They're also selling cold watermelon, fruit, and flavored ice cups, if anyone's interested."

Linda and Winnie perk up at the mention of the ice cups.

"We'll go," they answer as twins.

Because I spent the morning at the college, I'm not clamoring to go back but I don't want to stay in the house, either. Ruby will be napping and there's nothing to do.

I have a sudden idea. I can go down with them and then, disappear for a while to check on

White Cloud. I don't have a plan to stop him from going on the Vision Quest but maybe one will come to me when I see him again.

We all stir up the dust walking to the college. I pretend we're a lost ancient tribe looking for buffalo. I'm the scout charged with finding them. Twisting my head left and right, I scour the land for a sign of them.

"Anna, is something wrong with your neck?" asks Mom, with a worried frown.

"Um, no, I don't think so," I say, as I rub my neck. "It's just a little stiff from working on the records this morning."

It's not stiff at all. I'm just embarrassed to tell Mom I'm pretending to be a buffalo scout.

"Oren, she's working too hard at the college. She needs a break," Mom says, firmly.

Dad looks at me dubiously. "I'm not sure the work is that hard but if your neck hurts, Anna, rest it tomorrow."

At first, I think about the money I'll be losing for the cell phone, and I start to say," Dad, don't wor- ..."

Then I quickly decide a day off will give me plenty of time to figure out what I can do to help White Cloud. "Yes, Dad, a day off will help my neck."

It's hard to be me sometimes. The secret of the twig horse weighs me down. There's nothing I can do about it right now, though.

Chapter 14

Holy Man – *Wičháša Wakȟáŋ*

Everyone marches into the college. The artwork is set up in the rooms not used during the summer. It's not hard to separate myself from everyone else. Dad and Mom examine the sculptures lining the halls. Linda and Winnie, with a dollar each, go in search of ice cups. Vernon disappears into the photo display room and I head outside, again. I have the red pouch in my back pocket.

Circling the wall of the Lakota College, I find a recessed doorway. I hide in the shadows and take out the red pouch. Within seconds, the twig horse and I are on the grasslands of long ago. I see a thípi in the distance. *Time for a hike. It's hot. There are so few*

*trees here, although some grow by the river where
the camp has been set up.*

As I approach the village, I find myself trying
to tiptoe in. *Stop it, Anna,* I tell myself. *They can't
see or hear you. Remember, you are a ghost to them.*
Nothing has changed since I was here last. There
aren't signs of a big buffalo hunt. No meat hangs on
stick racks. No hides stretched to dry. Maybe the men
are still out scouting for buffalo herds.

I cross the space between the houses. There
he is. He drags long thin sticks to a space outside the
thípi and dumps them in a pile. White Cloud moves
slowly. His foot is bandaged today. I watch him sit
down in the dust and rub his foot.

Out of nowhere, Bright Star runs to the stack
of wood. "You won't do this, I won't let you," she
yells. She grabs the sticks and starts to fling them
away. *Yeah, Bright Star. Go, girl.*

An older native man emerges from a thipi
carrying a carved stick. He stands in front of White
Cloud and faces Bright Star. In a twist on my words,
he points the stick at Bright Star and says," Go, girl."

Bright Star is frustrated and angry. I hear her
thoughts, *What can I do to stop my younger brother
from this dangerous journey? Nothing. The Holy
Man approves. This will happen.*

I'm frozen in my spot. Now what do I do? I
watch and wait. White Cloud slowly gets up and
hobbles over to the scattered pile of sticks. He
arranges them into a bundle and counts them.

I can understand the Lakota language. He has sixteen sticks. He grunts in satisfaction. The older native stands and watches.

Bright Star makes a face at White Cloud. She turns quickly and stomps away. I know exactly how she feels. The adults rule the world and even though she's trying to save her brother, she has no say. I walk toward her and pat her shoulder. She stops and swivels her head. She sees nothing, so she turns her back and walks away. I'm amazed I have the power to touch. I think I can use this to help White Cloud but I still have no idea how. The Holy Man says, "This is where you will build the thípi." He moves his arm in a circle and walks away.

I decide to follow White Cloud. He works on building the sweat lodge. It begins to form before my eyes. White Cloud draws a circle with a stick. He bends the sixteen trees and lashes them together with strips of bark. He pounds several stakes into the ground. He covers the frame of the dwelling with hides. White Cloud steps back to look at his lodge. "Good," he says.

I think so, too. I thought he was done; but no, he piles and packs a mound of earth outside the skin door of the lodge. He drags rocks from a pile and sets them in a circle with more rocks in the center. Wood is stacked for burning. White Cloud carries rocks inside the sweat lodge. I walk through the doorway and see the shape of a fire pit in the center of the floor.

White Cloud crawls into a corner of the lodge. Exhausted by work, he falls asleep. Before I leave him to his rest, I take one more look. The wrapping on his foot has fresh blood on it.

It's time to head back to the college. I feel so discouraged. I want to find a way to help White Cloud but I have no plan. As an invisible person, he cannot hear or see me. My only advantage is I can hear his words and thoughts and I can use my body to cause movement but I've never experimented to see how much force I have. Can I pick up a rock? Can I grab hold of something and move it from place to place? I have no idea. It's clear to me that I must test my invisible powers.

I hurry out of the camp and head back the way I came. Along the way, I see rocks scattered about. I try to lift one of them. My hands go right through it. Next, I try a small stone. I attempt to pick it up and throw it. Nothing happens. Can't do it.

I take the hand I used to pat Bright Star's shoulder and place it on the side of the small stone and push. Surprise, the stone moves sideways. I do have this power to move small objects. Now, here's the question: Should I follow White Cloud on his Vision Quest? Is this small power enough to help the native boy when he is all alone on his journey?

With the help of the twig horse, I find myself back in the doorway of the college. I quickly close the red pouch and go in search of my tribe. I walk toward the front of the college. Linda and Winnie sit and talk on a low wall. Their mouths are stained blue. I guess they enjoyed their ice cups.

"Hi, girls. Where is everybody?" I inquire.

"Where did you go?" asks Linda. "We're ready to go and everyone is looking for you."

Winnie gives me her snake eyes. "Where were you?"

Oh, great, I must think fast. "You won't believe this," I begin.

Winnie keeps staring at me. *What is it with her?*

I continue, without looking at Winnie who makes me nervous. "As I said, you won't believe this."

"OK?" Winnie's smile plays on her lips while her eyes narrow.

"I took a walk around the college to see the bird design on the building, and I noticed a horse running down the road. It looked just like Red Paint. I thought he had escaped again." I pause for effect.

Linda exclaims, "No. No."

Winnie just stares and says nothing.

I reassure Linda, "I raced home to see if it was Red Paint. When I got there, I saw he was safely inside the gate. It was a different horse. So that's where I was."

Anxious to get Winnie's eyes off me, I quickly change the subject. "So, where is everybody now?

From around the corner, I hear voices say, "There she is,"

Mom reaches me first. "Anna, where have you been?"

Linda blurts out the whole story and it is a story.

"Thank you, Anna," says Vernon. "It's good you have your wits about you. All's well, that ends well, I always say."

"Yeah, I say that too," says Winnie. She gives me a look and turns away.

Vernon turns to our group. "Let's go home. Tonight is bonfire night."

I think about White Cloud's circle of rocks. I hope it's not bonfire night for him.

Chapter 15

Sweat Lodge – *Oínikağe*

The flames leap and dance. The bonfire is huge. Vernon set it up in a clearing on the side of the house. We all sit on log benches around it. The sky twinkles with stars. Into the darkness, little sparks of fire similar to tiny stars sail up and up. I could sit and watch it all night. It hypnotizes all of us into a comfortable silence. The only sound in the firelight is the crackle of the wood.

I wish we could have a bonfire at our New Jersey house but we can't. There are laws against it. Mom said years ago people could burn their fall leaves in their yards. Not anymore.

Winnie interrupts the silence. "Dad, are we going to send up our messages?"

"Sure, we can," agrees Vernon.

"What messages? What are we going to do?" asks Linda.

"We write a wish or a prayer on a piece of paper and put it into the fire," Vernon explains.

"Why?"

"The papers burn and the smoke with the prayer or wish goes up to the stars." Vernon winks at Linda.

"Do the wishes come true?" asks Linda.

"We'll have to try it and see," says Vernon.

"Is this a Lakota ritual?" I ask.

"No. It's a Sandoz ritual. Right, Winnie?" Vernon says. "I'll get some paper and pens for us." He goes into the house.

"I know what I'm going to wish for," declares Linda.

We all know what Linda wishes for. The question is, how big a pet does she want now?

Vernon returns and we all get busy writing our wishes on long strips of paper. I write: "I want to help White Cloud during his Vision Quest." Vernon collects the papers and, one by one deposits them into the flames. We watch the strips catch fire, burn and slowly rise in the air above the bonfire. The fire begins to die out. The darkness starts to close in.

Mom breaks the silence. "OK one and all, it's time for bed."

Winnie and Linda follow Mom into the house. The men and Ruby pour water on the remaining coals in the fire pit. As I sit on the log watching the embers fizzle out, I notice a half-burnt strip of paper lying on the ground. Someone's wish, I think. I scoop it up and read it. It says, "I wish Anna was my friend."

I don't have to study the handwriting to know whose wish this is. Winnie's. I am totally shocked. I don't know how to feel. I've spent so much time being annoyed at her I never considered the possibility of a friendship. Could I consider it now? I have to think about that.

The morning sunlight pours through the bedroom window. I stretch and sit up in bed. The bunk beds are empty. The house is quiet. I go into the kitchen. Breakfast dishes are piled in the sink. No one is around. The coffee machine is unplugged, but I see coffee still in the bottom of the pot. Umm, I decide to warm it up. It's delicious.

On the table is a written note. Sipping my mug of creamy, sugary coffee, I read it:

Dear Anna,
You were still sleeping when we left this morning. Dad is at work. The girls and I are at the rec center. Ruby has gone to the doctor with Vernon. I hope your neck is better. Get a good rest today.
Love, Mom

This couldn't be better. I have the whole day to myself. I swing into action. I gulp the coffee and get dressed. I'm outside with the red pouch in a matter of minutes. Today is the day I must figure out how to help White Cloud.

The little brown-twig horse speeds me on my way through time. Soon the village is in sight. I walk toward it. It's funny that everything is so quiet, just the same as at home. Are the people here? I move faster and soon see White Cloud's sweat lodge. I can hear voices coming from it. I slip inside.

White Cloud and native men sit in a circle around rocks which give off steamy smoke. It's extremely hot and dark in here. I recognize the Holy Man. Another man has a bucket of water. He pours water on the hot rocks. Steam rises. Each person says a prayer for White Cloud's journey. The Holy Man smokes the sacred pipe and passes it to the man on his left. White Cloud sits very still and waits as the pipe passes from one to another. At last it's his turn. More prayers follow. The Holy Man says the last prayer and leaves the lodge. Each member rises and does the same. As White Cloud exits the lodge, he says, "Now I will live again." I follow White Cloud out of the sweat lodge. *What now?* I guess I'll find out.

The Holy Man and White Cloud leave the village and the tribe behind as they walk toward the canyons in the Badlands.

I see a tearful Bright Star holding the hand of an older native woman as she watches her brother walk away. "I'm afraid I'll never see my brother again."

The older woman pulls Bright Star to her and hugs her. "The Great Spirit will guide him and watch over him. He will return to us."

Bright Star shakes her head. "White Cloud has a strong heart and he wants to be the same as all the other young men but he doesn't have a strong leg and foot. I am afraid for him."

I wish I could tell Bright Star I'll watch over her brother.

White Cloud, the Holy Man and I walk for hours over sandy, rocky land. A view of the Badlands Rock Mountains is always in sight. Finally, we reach our destination. Amazingly most of the Badlands are submerged canyons. Pink and beige rock cliffs with a red stripe snake through them. White Cloud and the Holy Man climb a cliff. The man faces the native boy and hands him the pipe. I inch closer to them. I can read their thoughts.

The Holy Man stares into White Cloud's eyes and thinks; *This is a boy of great courage. Great Spirit, protect him.*

I see White Cloud look deeply into the Holy Man's eyes and I hear his thoughts. *This Great Man of my tribe believes in me. I will complete my Vision Quest and return home.*

The Holy Man says some words then leaves. I notice White Cloud looks exhausted. He has extra bandages on his foot. He stands very still on the edge of the cliff, holding the pipe. He stares off into the distance.

I remember what I read about the Vision Quest. The seeker has to stand. This could last one day or four days. I say a prayer he gets his vision in one day. I can't stay here longer than today. I guess I could come back if it's longer but it would be harder to do. The sun beats down on us. I'm invisible. I don't need water. The sweat pours from White Cloud. He must be so thirsty. He never puts the pipe down. He stands stiff and straight like a soldier at attention. I sit down on a rocky ledge close to him. The hours drag on. Neither of us moves.

Suddenly, White Cloud calls out. He grabs his head and falls to his knees. I jump up. *This must be it.* I watch him carefully. He shakes his head from side to side. He begins to moan and breathe hard and fast. Then he falls to the ground and lies perfectly still. I go quickly to his side. *Is he OK?* I watch him open his eyes. He stays motionless on the ledge. He had his vision. I'm sure of it.

Then as quickly as he fell, he jumps up. Still holding the pipe, he begins to make his way off the cliff. His energy is amazing. I can hardly keep up. The way down is harder than the way up. Loose gravel and rock cause us to slip halfway down. He stops to rest on a narrow outcrop. I'm glad for the pause. Something catches his attention down the mountainside. White Cloud drops to his knees and lowers his head to see something further down. I follow his line of vision. Oh, no, climbing the rocks toward us is a mountain lion. The large tawny cat tests his paws on the rock edges to get a foothold up the side. As he climbs, bits of rock crumble and slide downward. He slips on the sides but continues to try ways to reach our ledge. White Cloud stands and starts to go back up. He tries to grab hold of some small bushes growing out of the cliff sides. As he pulls on the bushes, I watch them come apart in his hand. The mountain lion reaches a paw upward. He stretches to claw White Cloud's leg. It's his twisted leg. White Cloud moves up and hangs onto a protruding rock. He puts his foot under him.

Panic starts to build in me. *What to do? What to do?*

Chapter 16

Journey – *Oíčhimani*

The mountain lion is directly below White Cloud. The big cat stops and screams at him. I look around for something, anything I can use to help White Cloud. Directly in front of me is a large boulder but I can't move any large rocks. I've already tried.

Try again, I tell myself. I use the edge of my hand to move the sand and pebbles that hold the boulder in place. I press and dig in the space. I do this again and again. The boulder starts to move. There's only one direction it can go. Down, down. As it bumps against the side of the cliff, it gains speed. With an angry scream, the mountain lion attempts to jump out of the boulder's way. Too late. The boulder and the wild cat spin wildly in the air and fall to the bottom of the canyon.

White Cloud shakes all over. He takes deep breaths and sits down on the side of the cliff. He pulls his knees up and wraps his arms around them while he gently rubs his twisted foot. After a short rest, White Cloud peers down into the ravine. The mountain lion does not move. He begins his descent. I follow behind. We make our way back along the path to the village.

I am so happy no harm came to him. No one will ever know what I did to help him. It doesn't matter to me. I'm just proud of myself. *You did it, Anna,* I tell myself. At home, I don't feel brave at all. I'm usually afraid of many things. Well, now, I know I can be brave when it counts.

We trudge along together. An invisible girl, a ghost girl and a Lakota boy who carries in his heart the vision he just had. I wish I knew what he saw in his vision. We walk into the village. White Cloud heads toward the Holy Man's thípi. He calls to him and waits outside. The Holy Man tells him to enter. I go too. I know this is private between the two of them but I really want to know what the vision was.

They sit by the fire pit, which has no fire. White Cloud is quiet until the wise man waves his hand at him to begin talking. Then he begins his tale:

"Wičháša Wakȟáŋ, my journey, and task are completed. I stood on the cliff and waited for the spirits to come to me. They came with a great noise and a swirl of air. I didn't know what the thundering noise was. It traveled around and around me and wouldn't stop. I said my prayer to the Great Spirit and waited.

"The vision cleared. Before me were many, many animals, same as the big dog we found on the plains. They came to me. One put his large head on my shoulder. I was not afraid. I jumped on his back and held onto the hairs on his neck. I no longer felt the pain of my injured foot. I was able to move with speed as the Lakota men who have good feet. I felt strong as the many boys in our tribe. The big dog became my feet and legs.

"Wičháša Wakȟán, what does my vision mean?"

I hear what White Cloud says about his vision. I know exactly what it means. Horses have come to the Oglala Lakota.

"Holy Man, tell me the meaning of what I've seen."

The native man is silent. He sits completely still and closes his eyes. Several minutes pass before he raises his hand and begins to speak, "You have seen the future of the Oglala Lakota. The spirits have chosen you to lead our people to these big dogs. These big dogs will become your feet and will become the feet of our people.

"Our hunters and scouts will sit on these big dogs as we follow the buffalo from place to place. We no longer will be known as people who run after the buffalo. The Great Spirit has decided we will go after the buffalo with four legs instead of two. White Cloud, you must listen to the spirits carefully. They will show you the way. You will lead our people to a new life."

The Holy Man lights a pipe and passes it to White Cloud. After they smoke the pipe, White Cloud gets up and leaves. He walks through the village to his thípi. Bright Star sits by the cook pot.

When she spots her brother, she gasps and runs to him. Tears run down her cheeks as she hugs him to her.

"Are you all right?" She steps back to check him from top to bottom. Her eyes linger on his foot. "Are you all right?" she asks again.

White Cloud smiles at her. "I'm fine." They walk and talk as they head inside their thípi. I stand outside. I don't think it's right to go inside. This is their time together. White Cloud will explain what he saw to Bright Star.

Suddenly, I feel all alone. Invisible me can't talk to anyone about what I saw and heard. I must carry my secret inside my heart. I walk outside the village. It's time to go back to Pine Ridge. As I walk, I think about the task ahead of White Cloud.

Now that he's had his vision, the Holy Man said he must bring the "big dogs" to the people. How on earth can he do that?

I haven't seen any signs of horses around the village or the surrounding hills. Maybe the one big dog they found dead had come from far away. I try to relax. After all, the Holy Man said the spirits would lead White Cloud to the horses.

I calm myself. I've done my job to keep White Cloud safe on his Vision Quest. He had the vision. He's back to his sister, safe and sound. My job is done, I guess. Before I take hold of the twig horse, I look around at the land before me. I say a final goodbye. Goodbye to the ancient Lakota people. Goodbye to White Cloud and Bright Star. Goodbye to my secret adventure.

I'm back in seconds. I walk around the outside of the house. Red Paint is in his yard. He whinnies at me. As I walk closer to him, he nods his head up and down and uses one hoof to paw at the ground.

I really am afraid of horses. They are so big and can rear up and be wild. I could get trampled by them. Red Paint snorts at me. What does that mean? I have no idea. He hangs his head over the fence. I get a little closer. Horses have such big teeth. I'm sure a bite would hurt. I put my hand out to touch his nose. He stands very still and lets me. His nose feels soft like Linda's favorite old stuffed bunny. He stares into my eyes. He's trying to tell me something. *What does he want?* I wonder. Maybe he wants a carrot. I go into the shed to get the bag of carrots stored there. When I offer him the biggest one, he turns his head. He doesn't want it.

"Well, suit yourself. I don't know what you're trying to tell me. Winnie will be home soon. You work it out with her. I don't know horse talk."

With that said, I turn to head into the house. Red Paint whinnies and kicks a board on the fence.

Horses, I think, are not big dogs. They are trouble.

Chapter 17

Help – *Woókiye*

The house is empty and still. I wonder if I have time to put on a pot of coffee before everyone comes thundering back.

In the kitchen, I reach for an apple. I'm starving. Running the water for the coffee pot, I think back over the day's events. What an adventure it was, I'm glad I'm here in Pine Ridge. If I were home in New Jersey, the only excitement would be walking the dogs, going to the pool and listening to Liz go on and on about Jason.

Car doors slam. Voices tumble toward me. They're back. I quickly dump out the coffee pot. No coffee today.

Winnie and Linda find me first.

"How's your neck?" asks Linda. She gives me a hug.

Little sisters can be sweet. I had forgotten all about my neck "excuse". "It's much better. Thank you, Linda."

Winnie gives me the snake look and smirks. "I'll bet it is."

This is the same girl who wrote on her wish paper she wants to be my friend. I can't figure her out. I think it's better to stay away from her.

Mom arrives weighted down with swim tubes, towels and an empty picnic basket. "Anna, how are you feeling?"

"My neck is back to normal, Mom." I turn my head from side to side to show her.

"Good. Anna, there's more stuff out in the car. Can you lend a hand?"

I help carry in pool things and some grocery bags. Linda and Winnie have gone into Ruby's room. I can hear the jingle of the Lakota dress. It's dress-up time again.

I need some time alone. Outside I sit on the bench and watch Red Paint. He must hear Winnie. He's pacing back and forth along the side of the fence. He stops and calls with a soft whinny. I laugh. He's calling Winnie with a whinny. She can't hear him from inside the bedroom.

I wonder how White Cloud will find what he calls the big dogs. With his sore foot, he can't wander around the plains or the Badlands endlessly searching for horses and, suppose he comes across a herd of horses; how does he bring them back to the village? Can he even get up on one with his bad leg? How does he figure out how to ride a horse?

Maybe the answers lie with the Spirits. He had the vision. They sent it to him. So, they must be going to help him with the rest of the Quest but something troubles me about all of it.

Something doesn't make sense but what is it?

I lean forward on the bench and watch Red Paint circle his fenced yard. He stops again at the gate and stares at me. He paws the ground. *Is he trying to tell me something?*

"What, Red Paint? What is it?" I whisper. My thoughts are disrupted with the banging of the back door. Winnie and Linda explode into the backyard. They yell, giggle, and push each other as they ignore me and head over to Red Paint.

"Anna, can you come in and help make dinner? Dad, Vernon, and Ruby will be home soon," Mom calls out from the kitchen window.

"Coming," I promise myself I'll think about White Cloud later. Something is troubling me but I'm not sure what it is.

Dinner talk is all about the weekend powwow. The girls are so excited. They interrupt each other and everyone with talk about the big day.

"Grandma, some of the bells are loose on my dress."

"Winnie, I didn't see any…" Linda starts.

"Winnie, I saw them, and I'm going to…" begins Ruby.

"I think we should…" Vernon tries to talk.

"Calm down, everyone," says Mom in her no-nonsense voice. "Let's talk one at a time. Vernon, you go first."

"Thank you, Maisie. As I was about to say, I think we should decide what time we're going to the powwow and which competitions and games we're going to enter. Pass the salad, please."

Everyone pauses for a second then the babbling fills the kitchen again.

"OK, let's have quiet from the children," directs Dad.

I hope he's not talking about me. I'm not a child. The only noisy children I hear are Winnie and Linda. I eat my salad and softly crunch the lettuce.

"Vernon, why don't you fill us in on what you recommend?" suggests Dad.

"OK. I think we should get there early for good seats. The powwow is set up in front of the Lakota College. The arena is a circle with a partial roof over the bleachers to give shade from the sun. There will be a special prayer to start the powwow. Everyone stands and joins in. After that comes the ceremonial procession, followed by native dancing to the drums. Winnie and I will wear our Lakota clothes and join the tribe for this."

Linda smiles and interrupts. "Are you going to wear a chief outfit?"

"I'm not a chief but the clothes are very special." Vernon continues, "When the dancing is finished the competitions will start. There will be watermelon, lemon and hot pepper eating contests. People are grouped by age. After the contests are over the games begin. There's a sign-up sheet for players to choose which games to join."

"Tell about the best part," urges Ruby.

"I know what you're thinking of," answers Vernon. "After dancing, competing and games, what do you think everyone wants?"

Vernon looks around the table.

Linda yells, "Ice cream," She hops with excitement in her seat.

"Well, that might come last, for sure but to start with everyone would want a good Lakota dinner cooked by some of the finest cooks at Pine Ridge."

"This is going to be the best day ever," announces Linda.

After cleaning up the kitchen, Mom and I join the others outside. The firepit holds a small fire tonight. The stars make a twinkling blanket over our heads. I should be feeling content and happy. After all, I accomplished my goal to keep White Cloud safe on his Vision Quest but there's a little worry worm in my brain making me feel as if I've missed something important. *What is my problem?*

Later at night, when everyone is settled in their beds, I close my eyes and review everything that happened. I relive all the events of the past few days. I let the worry worm have full rein over my thoughts.

Suddenly, I sit up in my bed. There it is, as plain as day or night. My worry. A certain knowledge floods through me. White Cloud would have died on his Vision Quest without me. The mountain lion certainly would have attacked and killed him.

Without my help and special powers, White Cloud *would not have made it safely back to his village.*

Maybe I, Anna Čhetáŋ, Lakota native, am one of the spirit guides sent to help White Cloud. Does it matter that I am not from the past but instead from the future? I am a ghost in his present. I am a spirit there to help him.

White Cloud still needs my help. If he is to bring the horses to the Lakota people, he will need a spirit guide.

My work is not done. Now, how do I do it?

Chapter 18

Friend – Girl to Girl – *Máške*

In the morning, Dad and I head down to the college. I have to work today. The vision of my cell phone dances in my head.

Back in the records room, I look for other files on Dad's list. The list includes "Black Hills" and "the Badlands." These lands are sacred to all the Lakota. I find these files in the cabinet's bottom drawer. As I pull out the file on the Badlands, an old map slides out and flutters to the floor. I scoop it up.

These are the same Badlands I visited yesterday with White Cloud. Of course, he lived hundreds of years ago, so there are bound to be some changes resulting from weather and time from when these maps were made. Still, an idea starts forming in my head. I wonder if this map would help me find horses. I have to think how.

The file on the Black Hills also includes an old map of the area. This might be useful too. I can't just remove files from the room, though. As I sit and think what to do, I hear the copier running in the outside office. Bingo, I grab the folders with the two maps and leave the room. When I get to the copier, I stand behind the older lady I've seen before. I give her my best "I'm-working-hard-for-my-dad" smile.

"Dear, do you want me to run some copies for you?" she asks, reaching for my folders.

I panic, and I don't know why. I just don't want anyone to guess what I'm doing and, of course, they wouldn't but I'm not thinking straight. "Thank you but my dad showed me how to use the copier," I reply as I hold the folders tight to my chest.

"OK, dear. If you need help, just come to my desk."

I do know how to run copies. My mom taught me how so I could help her with the orders at Čhetáŋ's Nursery. After I make the map copies, I return and work in the records room. I want to earn my cell phone money honestly. No more working for White Cloud. The morning passes quickly. Dad and I return to the house for lunch.

Everyone is in the kitchen and what a mess it is. The counters are covered with bowls and spoons. The sink is filled with measuring cups and pans. The oven is on, and all the burners on top have bubbling pots. Ruby calls out directions as she waves a wooden spoon. "It's time to check the soup. Give it a good stir, so nothing sticks to the bottom. Maisie, open the oven door. We don't want the chokeberry cake to burn."

"Well, well, what's going on here? Whatever it is, it all smells delicious but I think this is too much food for lunch," jokes Dad. He chuckles.

Linda adjusts her apron. "Dad, this isn't for lunch. We're making food to take to the powwow tomorrow. Ruby knows how to cook good Lakota food."

Linda is a friend to the obvious. No one even says, "I know that."

After we eat lunch, clean up, and wrap up the powwow food to store in the refrigerator, everyone moves on to other activities. The girls are outside grooming Red Paint. Mom and Dad are reading in the living room. Ruby rests in her room, and Vernon talks softly on the phone.

I go to the bedroom where I've hidden the maps of the Black Hills and Badlands. Studying them doesn't help me think of a plan to help White Cloud find and get some horses for his tribe.

I need some more information on wild horses and where they can be found. I am now convinced the discovery of the dead horse, big dog, means there are other horses in the area; but where would they be? Would they hide in the Black Hills covered with forests and pine trees? Or would they head to the Badlands and hide in the many canyons and rocky nooks? I hate to say this but I'm going to need Winnie's help.

Leaving the house, I head for the girls. They're brushing Red Paint's mane. Winnie watches me approach them. "Is something wrong?" she asks.

"No. Why would something be wrong? I just thought I'd hang out with you girls."

Winnie raises her eyebrows and gives a shrug. "Whatever you want to do. I thought you didn't like horses." She hands her brush to Linda and turns to face me squarely. Her eyes have that squinty look again. She doesn't trust me. I haven't earned it. This isn't going to be easy.

"I am scared of horses but since I've been here with you and your family, I see how gentle Red Paint is. He doesn't bite or rear up. He seems to be a genuinely nice horse."

"He's a great horse," says Linda.

"Winnie, if you don't mind teaching me, I'd love to learn more about horses." I walk over to the horse and rub his nose.

"Why? Soon you'll be leaving here and you won't have one in New Jersey," responds Winnie.

Linda jumps right in. "Maybe we will get one. We can keep him at the garden center. Mom has lots of sheds there. I'll go over after school every day and ride him."

"I don't see what the point is," says Winnie.

I take that for a "no". I persist. "Winnie, you're right. Soon we'll all be gone. I've had a great time here but you and I haven't spent any time together. I've been working and you've been with Linda. I just think it would be nice for you and me to do something together before we go."

"Really, Anna?" asks a doubtful Winnie.

"Yes, really," and I mean it.

"OK. I've taught Linda a lot. I guess we'll have to start from the beginning," Winnie says. "This is the bridle and this…"

"First, let's sit down." I point to the bench. "I have some basic questions about horses." *It's now or never,* I think. "Are there wild horses around here?"

Winnie looks surprised at my first question. "Um, not now. There used to be a long time ago."

Now we're cooking. "Winnie, were they in the Black Hills or the Badlands?"

"They lived in the Badlands in corners of the canyons where no one could see them," she says and smiles, "but Lakota are excellent trackers and they were found."

"Did the Lakota from long ago have to capture the horses with ropes?" I can't think of how else you could drag these big creatures into the village.

Winnie laughs out loud. "Anna, you don't know much of anything about horses."

"I give up. You're right. How did they capture them?"

"Well, first, one of the braves tames one horse to ride. Then, he goes out searching for the herd. They move around just as do buffalo. After finding it, the brave captures another horse using a rope. After that, it isn't hard. He goes back to the herd with another brave. Waving ropes in the air and making loud whooping cries they chase the herd to the village and into a pen built to hold the horses. The people run out and close the pen. That's how it's done.

Anna, are you going to look for wild horses?" asks a confused Winnie. "What would you do with them?"

"She'd give them to me," says Linda. She runs to hug me.

"I would, Linda, but they won't fit in the car for the ride home." I hug her back. "Winnie, what you said about the first brave finding a horse, which one did he pick from the herd?" This seems an important question.

"Easy. The herd consists of all females. The stallion is the head horse and guards the herd. The brave avoids him at all costs. He looks through the herd to find the female who is a little slower than the rest and maybe older. This horse won't put up much of a fight. That's his horse."

"Horse capturing is complicated," I say.

Winnie nods. "Do you want to ride on Red Paint?"

Oh, no, I'm not ready for this; but my mouth says, "Sure. Can you show me how to get up on him?"

We go through the gate door. Winnie starts her instruction. "Come to the side of him. There's no saddle, so you'll ride bareback." She leads me to the neck of the horse. "Now grab hold of his mane and jump up. Swing your leg over his back."

I do everything she says. My heart beats so fast. I think it will pop out of my chest.

Linda yells, "Go, Anna. you can do it."

I do it right. I grab, I hold, I swing, and I sail through the air and land with my face on the ground. I'm on the other side of Red Paint. "Ow, Ow," I howl.

Winnie and Linda howl, too but with laughter.

I brush myself off. "Let's try again."

"Instead of grabbing his mane, grab his withers," says Winnie.

"Where's that?" I ask.

"The bottom of his neck."

I try that move. It works. I'm up on a horse.

"Ta-dah, Now how do I steer him?"

"Use the mane and direct him with your thighs."

I say, "Giddy-up." I follow Winnie's directions. It works. I'm riding a horse. Red Paint walks slowly around the fence. When I'm back in front of Winnie, I ask, "How do I get down?"

"Just swing your leg over and slide off."

I swing my leg and slide and again crash on the ground. Linda and Winnie hold their stomachs laughing. I brush the dirt off my face, my hair, my arms, my stomach and say, "Thanks, Winnie. That was fun." I walk back into the house.

Mom looks up from her book. "Anna, you're covered with dirt. Go take a shower."

"I know, Mom. The things we do for others."

Chapter 19

Family – *Thiwáhe*

Powwow day dawns sunny and warm. With my head still on the pillow, I can hear the hustle and bustle in the outer rooms. There are costumes to be gathered, food to be transported, schedules to be determined and plans to be made. It will be a busy day.

Still, I lie in my bed. My head fills with worries about White Cloud. Yesterday, I was so sure I wouldn't see White Cloud again. My work was done. Now I'm so sure I have to go back and help him find the horses he saw in his vision. While everyone else plans for the powwow, I make a plan to go back to a village, hundreds of years in the past.

Linda comes charging into the bedroom. "Wake up, Sleepyhead. Today is the best day ever. Do you want to try the watermelon-eating contest? Winnie and I do. We don't want to try the lemon or hot pepper contests. There are races too. Do you think I can win a race? Do you know what the prizes are? Money, I want to win some. I'm saving for a horse, you know."

"Slow down, Linda." I sit up in bed and stretch. "I agree with you. It's going to be a fun day. Let me get dressed, please."

I see Dad writing at the kitchen table. He looks up. "Good morning, Anna. Have you heard from Linda yet? Today is the big day." He laughs.

I drink some poured orange juice and look longingly at the filled coffee pot. "I think all of Pine Ridge can hear Linda. What time does it start?"

"We should be in our seats at 1 o'clock. The Grand Entrance is at one-thirty; but I'm going to the college this morning to help them set up the speakers and drums and do some other things."

Hmmm, I think. *This is my chance to help White Cloud.* "I could go with you to help set up the food tables and stuff."

"I think that's great, Anna," says Dad, pushing away from the table.

After a bite of breakfast, I'm off to the college with Dad.

I've stuffed my red pouch and the map of the Badlands into my back pocket. Here I go. At the college, Dad and I separate. I find my shadowy doorway and pull out the twig horse. I don't know why but I give it a little kiss. Maybe for luck?

Before I take my journey, I study the Badlands map. It's hard to understand. The rock canyon walls twist and turn. Horses could be in any corner. I just have to take a chance I'll find them. I hold the twig horse with both hands and swirl through time. The twig horse and I are back outside the village. Nothing else can come with me—no red pouch, no map—just Ghost Anna and her magic horse.

I have a lot to do here in a short time. I must be back before the powwow starts. I run to the village. I need to find White Cloud. Stopping at the Holy Man's thípi, I look inside. No one. White Cloud's thípi is straight ahead. Bright Star sits outside with an older woman. Their heads are bent as they sew tiny beads onto a piece of leather.

The older woman asks, "How long has he been gone?"

Bright Star answers, "Since morning."

"Did he take food for his journey?"

"Yes. He said he won't come back alone."

"What does that mean?"

"He plans to search in the Badlands until he finds the big dogs in his vision." She sighs and sets down her sewing. "I pray the Great Creator will help him on this quest."

I don't have a second to lose. I head toward the Badlands. My only good luck is White Cloud's bad luck. His foot prevents him from traveling fast. If I hurry, I can find him.

The sun beats down on all living things. I almost wish I had a horse to ride. I would have caught up to him by now. I don't know in which direction he's walking. I'm hoping he's taking the same path he took for the Vision Quest. I pick up my speed.

Around a curve, I almost stumble over him. White Cloud is asleep on the ground with his head under a bush for the shade. I make a quick decision. I'll leave him here and search for the horses myself. When and if I find them, I'll lead him to them.

I trek over the rocky cliffs and into the canyons. I check out every corner I find. No horses. The hiking tires me. I check the position of the sun. It's overhead. That means it's noon. I have to hurry. I pick up my pace. I look as I run. Nothing. The sun moves downward. My time here is over. I have to go back.

I take the twig horse in my two hands. In seconds I'm back in the doorway. I return to a different scene. The college campus buzzes with noise. People walk toward the benches. Children play in the field. Many natives begin to dress in their ceremonial clothes. They put them on over shorts and tee-shirts. Some men work together to mark lines on a field with chalk. I spy Linda by the benches. She helps Winnie with her jingle dress and shawl.

I call to them. "Hi, girls. Where's Mom and Dad?"

Linda points to a group of men and women. Vernon is nearby in full Lakota outfit called regalia. He looks the same as a chief. I sit on the bench to wait for the parade to start. I can't help but feel sad and disappointed. I want to help White Cloud. If he can find the horses then life will change for his tribe.

What can I do now? I won't be able to get away until tomorrow. Maybe. If I go back and if he is still looking for the horses, maybe I can help. That's a lot of "ifs and maybes." I sigh.

"What's the matter, Anna? Not ready for a powwow?" asks Mom, as she sits down next to me.

"Nothing's wrong. It's just been a long day. By the way, I see everyone but Ruby. Where is she?" I ask.

Mom makes a sad face. "The doctor advised her not to come. He said her leg is healing nicely but she shouldn't put pressure on it. She wasn't happy. Sometimes we have to do hard things so other things get better."

I think about my useless trip into the canyon this morning and revise Mom's words: You can do hard things and sometimes nothing gets better.

Linda and Dad join us. There's a buzz in the crowd. The parade starts. I watch the proud people enter the arena. The clothes are beautiful. Most have bright red, yellow, black, green and other colors all in one outfit. The women and girls wear the jingle dresses. Many of the women and bigger girls have fringed shawls draped across their shoulders. The native men and boys wear soft skin breeches. They have eagle feather bustles and head roaches. Beaded cuffs and bags are attached to their clothes.

The chief says the prayer. The drums keep up a strong rhythm for the dancers. I feel hypnotized as I watch. The dance and the people stir a deep feeling of pride in me.

I whisper to Dad, "Here, we're all native people. We're connected."

Dad looks down at me and says, "You're growing up, Anna. That's part of what 'Bridge the Divide' means."

"Look," squeals Linda, "There's Winnie."

Winnie looks toward the bleachers. She smiles and continues her dance. The chief praises the dancers for their efforts. He speaks in Lakota and then English. With a wave of his hand and a flourish of his microphone, he announces the start of the contests and games. Lots of young men hurry to the chalked-off fields for a game of native stickball.

"Young people between the ages of five and eight come to the field for our watermelon-eating contest," announces the judge.

Winnie runs to us on the benches. She pulls at Linda's hands. "Let's go, Linda."

We watch the kids line up and face the judge. Each of them is handed a large piece of watermelon. I can tell Linda is scared. She's shaking her whole body back and forth. Winnie must be an old hand at this. She's calm and ready. The judge counts to three in Lakota. The chomping begins. Everyone takes giant bites. Juice runs down small chins. Then it's over and one child steps to the front with a raised hand. We stand and cheer. It's Winnie. She turns and hugs a sticky Linda and goes to collect her prize. Linda jumps for joy. They hold hands and run back to us.

"Congratulations, Winnie," we all say.

Winnie holds her five-dollar prize in the air. "This is for Linda. She's saving for a horse."

I think *Winnie has a big heart. She knows how to be a good friend.*

We watch the rest of the contests and the games. I don't know the teams, so I cheer for both sides. We all head to the food tables and get plates of native food. Mom and Vernon spread a blanket on the ground and we sit together. It's as if we're one big family. Back at the house, we all stop to check on Ruby. She seems tired and bored in her room. Mom hands her a plate of powwow food.

"Tell me everything," Ruby says as she dips her fork into the meat-covered fried bread.

"Winnie danced with her mom's shawl. She was really good," offers Linda.

Ruby drops her fork. "I wish I could have been there."

Winnie jumps up and hugs her grandma. "I'll dance now for you, Grandma."

Mom says, "Let's leave and give Winnie some space for her dance." She herds us all out of the small room.

Everyone goes to the living room. I turn into my room but soon leave. I stand outside Ruby's room and watch Winnie do her dance. She dances in total silence. It's beautiful. I can hear the drum music in my head. The shawl sways in the air. Winnie moves gracefully in the small space. She bends, bows, floats. Then she stops. Ruby holds out her arms to her. Winnie climbs on the bed and throws the shawl up in the air. It comes gently down and covers Ruby and Winnie as a tent. I hear soft murmurs and a giggle under the blue shawl.

I walk to my room.

Today was the worst of times and the best of times.

Chapter 20

Joy – *Wówiyuškiŋ*

No work today. It's the weekend. At the breakfast table, the conversation centers on the plans for today. I listen and move my eggs around my plate. I'm feeling glum. I'm sure it's going to be one of those days when I'll have to tag along with the group. We'll go see a national park or something. I won't be able to use the twig horse. I keep picturing White Cloud wandering around the Badlands searching for the horses. He won't have anyone to help him. Meaning me, of course.

I half listen to what the adults say. Then my ears prick up.

"We should take it easy today," says Mom. "Yesterday was fun but so busy. I think we need some downtime. If we take a trip, we'll have to leave Ruby behind again. That's two days in a row."

"I agree," says Vernon. Dad nods his head.

"Linda, we could ride Red Paint to a picnic area and have a picnic," says Winnie.

Linda asks, "Could I sit up front on Red Paint and steer him?"

"Sure," says Winnie and turns to her dad. "Dad, I taught Linda and Anna how to ride Red Paint. I'm a very good teacher."

"Winnie, it's not our Lakota custom to brag about ourselves. We're taught that humility in all things is the Lakota way. Do you know how our chiefs are chosen?"

"No," answers Winnie.

"We choose the humblest among us. That person will care about the people and will work to do his best not for praise but for the good of all," finishes Vernon.

"OK. I won't brag about myself again," says Winnie.

Linda pipes up, "But you are the best riding teacher ever and I say so."

Everyone laughs. Chairs scrape back from the table as the day's plans are discussed. Dad's going to help Vernon with the outdoor chores. Mom wants to work on the laundry. Ruby will do some sewing. And me? I announce I want to take a long walk to explore the area around the college. Well, it's sort of true. I'll just do the exploring in White Cloud's time.

I get dressed and head out. I'm down at the college and then back outside White Cloud's village in minutes. I put the twig horse in my pocket. Here I go again. It's probably my last chance to do this. White Cloud can't stay out in the canyons looking for horses. He'll need water and food. I have to help him find the herd.

I follow the same path as before. I've traveled it so much it feels like a path at home. I walk quickly. After what seems hours, I catch sight of White Cloud. He slips, slides and grabs onto shrubs as he descends a steep canyon. I do the same.

At the bottom, everything looks the same as at the top. I don't see any signs of a herd. White Cloud continues to walk but at a slow pace. His foot must hurt because he leans his weight on his other leg.

Suddenly, he stops and kneels on the ground. I watch him pick something up, examine it then throw it to the ground.

He begins to move faster through the canyon. Behind him, I reach the spot where he knelt. I see what he threw down. It was a long clump of golden hair. It isn't native hair. It has to be from a horse. He's on the right trail. I start to feel excited and a little nervous. I don't quite have a plan ready for when we get to the horses. I hope a plan pops into my head.

As White Cloud moves ahead, he scans the ground for more signs of horses. We walk for a long time before he stops again. White Cloud stands still. He listens. I hear it too. Hoof beats. Then a cloud of dust heads our way. *Here they come*. Right toward us. White Cloud looks as surprised as I am. We run to some rocks and crouch down behind them. The horses gallop past and take a left to the other side of the canyon wall. White Cloud jumps up and follows. Me too. We hike along the path made by the herd. It drops down into another part of the canyon, almost invisible from where we are. There they are. The horses have made a home in a part of the canyon with some trees, grass and a little pond.

White Cloud crouches down to watch them. I can hear his thoughts. He's wondering what to do next. I reach into my pocket and pull out the twig horse. I hold it out to him. It floats in the air between us. He can't see my invisible hand and arm, extending the horse to him. He cringes and moves backward. I move the twig horse closer. He sees it's in the shape of a horse and thinks it's a sacred item brought to him from the spirits. He touches it and immediately can see me.

"Who are you? Are you the spirit of my ancestors come to help me?" he asks.

Well, I am a native. Not from the past but from the future. "Yes," I say.

He looks relieved. "How can I bring these big dogs to my village?"

I remember everything his future descendant, Winnie, taught me. "We have to search in the herd and find an older gentle mare to ride. This big dog is the first. When you can ride it, you can come back with another man and bring the rest of the big dogs to your village."

"Spirit of my people show me what to do."

I motion with my hand for him to follow me. Now I'm in the lead. Not a spot I love. I must get this right.

Off to the side of the herd stands a small white-and-brown horse. She nibbles at the grass on the edge of the pond. I point for White Cloud to hide behind a tree. Invisible me heads for the horse. Of course, I know that animals can see me. But she stands quietly eating the grass and doesn't look up until I'm directly in front of her.

I rub her nose and whisper to her. "Don't be afraid. I need you to trust me. Come with me to help the Lakota. You'll be the first one to come to the village."

I pull on her withers and swing my leg over her back. She bucks and tries to throw me off. The small horse twists and jumps in her efforts to dislodge me. I hang on tightly. I can't let go. This is my only chance and I will succeed. The other horses whinny and begin to run out of the canyon. She tries to follow her herd. I bend over her head and hang onto her mane. Pressing my legs on her back I steer her away from the herd and back to the hidden canyon. I talk softly to her. "It's OK. It's OK."

Back in the canyon, she slows to a walk. I pat her sides and pull her to a stop. White Cloud runs to us from behind the tree. He comes right to the horse and gently rubs her nose. I hold out the twig horse so that we can connect again.

Thank you, Spirit. You have helped me fulfill my vision. My people and I will be forever grateful.

I slide off the horse without falling on my face. I think Linda is right; Winnie is a great teacher.

"I can show you how to ride this big dog then you can go back to your village."

"Is it hard?"

This time I'm not going to lie. "It's hard but you've done harder things."

I show him how to mount the horse. He does it without falling off. He sits in the front and I explain how to steer the horse with his legs. I start to congratulate myself on my teaching then I remember Vernon's words on humility. With both of us on the horse we head toward the village. Before we get there, I say, "Stop here. I want to get off."

"Don't you want to come with me?" he asks.

"You ride in by yourself." White Cloud nods. I slide off the horse and watch him go.

The natives see him from a distance. They begin to run toward him. They are shouting, laughing and waving their hands at him. White Cloud surprises them all and gallops fast past them. They give a loud cheer. He turns the horse around and gallops back. He brings the horse to a standstill in front of the crowd. They reach up to touch him and the horse.

Bright Star smiles from ear to ear. She says to him, "You did it,"

White Cloud looks at his sister.

He says, "I have my feet back."

Chapter 21

Life – *Wičoŋi*

I carefully wrap up the twig horse in a paper towel and gently put it in the side pocket of my suitcase. It's time to pack up and leave Pine Ridge. I'm surprised to find I feel sad to go. I didn't want to come here and now I don't want to leave. I can't say I'll miss White Cloud and Bright Star. They had gone from here a long time ago. It's the Sandozes who I'll miss.

When I came back to the house after my final trip to see White Cloud, Winnie was waiting for me in our bedroom. I walked in dusty and tired. She didn't ask me where I had been. She walked toward me, smiling, and without saying a word, she hugged me. Then she said, "Thank you."

"For what?" I asked, instantly worried she knew about the twig horse and White Cloud.

Winnie shook her head, smiled again and walked out of the room. That was all. I was afraid to ask another question. Is it possible she knows what happened with the twig horse? I'll never know the answer.

I hear both families say goodbye. I push my suitcase in front of me and join everyone in the kitchen. Ruby gives Mom a lunch for us to take. Winnie and Linda stand with their arms around each other and tissues in their hands. Vernon shakes Dad's hand. Vernon opens the front door.

We all stand in the front yard next to a fully packed car. It's time to go home. I look at the little house. So much has happened since we first entered it. It isn't the mansion Winnie described. *It's not filled with toys and electronics. There's no cool pool in the backyard. Instead, it's filled with people who love each other and who are good to their friends.*

Dad drives slowly out of Pine Ridge. We're all quiet.

Linda starts to cry. Wiping tears off her face with her hand, she says, "I already miss everyone. I really miss Winnie and Red Paint. Can we drive back and stay here?"

Dad pulls to the side of the road and shuts off the engine. He turns to talk to Linda. "Honey, we all miss the Sandozes. They are a wonderful family but they're not gone forever. Vernon promised me he would bring Ruby and Winnie to New Jersey for a long visit and I heard Winnie tell Anna she would call once a week."

Linda smiles. "Will they bring Red Paint too?"

"I don't think so but nothing is saying we can't come back next summer for another visit. The Lakota College wants me to come back to teach."

He starts up the engine and pulls out. We head to the gas station. Mom and Linda get out of the car to buy some drinks at the mini-mart. I stand next to Dad as he pumps gas.

My eye catches the bumper of the car. There is the sticker Dad put on in New Jersey, **Bridge The Divide**. I think about the meaning of it. It means a coming together, the past and the present, old cultures and new cultures, your tribe and my tribe. Everyone moving forward together. I get it.

With my twig horse, I lived it.

That's my secret. Please don't tell anyone my story.

Endnote

The Lakota people are proud, strong people, descendants from ancient tribes. They lived for centuries throughout the plains in the middle of America. Following the buffalo herds, camping near rivers, and gathering plants gave them everything they needed for a good life. They took only what they needed and thanked the Great Spirit for everything.

Throughout the book, Anna Čhetáŋ, a Lakota native becomes a student as she learns Lakota history from her father and the Sandoz family. She discovers connections between ancient people and present-day people. The history and customs, she discovers, tell the story of the Lakota people.

The story of the Lakota people finding horses in the 1700s is historically accurate. They did, at first, call them "big dogs."

The places she visits with her family are open to the public.

Horse
Photo by David Dilbert

About the Authors

The authors of this book worked together to bring a story of Lakota culture and history to all children, both native and non-native.

Philomine Lakota and Carol Morosco are the same age. They are teachers and grandmothers. Philomine is a native Lakota who teaches language and culture to the students of Red Cloud School in South Dakota. Carol Morosco is a non-native retired teacher who worked in Virginia schools for many years.

They came together to write an historical fiction book featuring words from the Lakota language. It's their hope this book reaches children from all backgrounds and cultures and fosters an understanding and appreciation of our many similarities and differences.